LACE LAMENTS

/ / / /

J.R. RAIN
&
H.P MALLORY

THE HAVEN HOLLOW SERIES

Wanda's Witchery

Published by
Rain Press

Copyright © 2023 by J.R. Rain & H.P. Mallory

All rights reserved.

Printed in the United States of America.

ISBN- 9798861125604

Chapter One

My shop was full of customers, and I was one more shrill giggle away from hexing myself deaf.

Of course, the instant the gaggle of werewolf females started pouring through the door of Wanda's Witchery, I'd known I was in for it. My cousin Maverick, who watched the shop during daylight hours, had taken one look and made a rapid retreat. The louse. I made a mental note to pay him back for that little bit of cowardice. Sure, it was my store, but he could have stayed for moral support.

From what I could overhear from their conversation, the entire crowd seemed to be related to each other in various ways. Judging from the age range (between bent-over/ can hardly walk to toddler), at least four generations were crammed into my limited floor space between the racks and the mannequins. That didn't surprise me, because werewolves tended to settle down young, and have big litters. Huge families were the norm.

Ick.

It wasn't that I didn't get crowds in my store (though most people didn't seem to want any witnesses when they were buying enchanted clothing, especially of the losing weight variety), but werewolves, in my mind, were of the more unsavory sort of supernatural. Now, before you think I'm the supreme bitch of bitches, I didn't give a spell that they turned into wolves (aside from the fact that they did have a distinctive dog odor). No, the reason I turned my nose up was completely owing to the fact that werewolves trained their females almost from birth to be cringing and submissive. Female werewolves wanted nothing more than to get married and pump out babies, and that was something I couldn't tolerate. Women were more than our ability to breed. Furthermore, I'd been brought up to believe the exact opposite regarding a woman's place in the world—witches didn't believe in marriage, and while we did have children, they tended to be raised by the entire coven. That way, they were never one poor frazzled woman's concern, but everyone's.

Though, considering I was both married (and to a vampire, no less) and childless—well, unless you counted Sybil, but the mannequin that Maverick and I brought to life accidentally was really more of a niece to me—I didn't have a lot of high ground from which to sneer down.

Still, the horrible combination of excited chatter and timid hesitation to express an opinion was going to cause me to climb the walls in another fifteen seconds. I did want to make a sale, though. Alas, the perils of owning a small business.

I tried to surreptitiously glance out the front window to see if there were any lights on in Poppy's Potions, across the street. If my Gypsy BFF was still working, maybe I could send up a distress signal, and she'd come over and speak her native language of inane cheeriness at my customers until they went away, or preferably, bought something and went away.

But the lights were out, and the store closed. And that meant I was on my own, with only my fraying patience to keep me from 'accidentally' cursing the whole group to lose their voices or something similar.

I should have known. Poppy kept to daylight hours, and considering how late the sun set this time of year, even staying open for increased tourist traffic in Haven Hollow would have seen her home ages ago. It was just one of the many irritations of my having to pretend to be a vampire. Really, I was lucky to have Maverick to watch the store during the day, though I'd have rather eaten live toads than ever admit as much to him. That was just the sort of relationship we had.

As to why I was a witch pretending to be a vampire? Story time! Once upon a time, my idiot husband, Lorcan Rowe, had witnessed a car accident and pulled the ravishing, dark-haired driver from the wreckage. Now, while the woman was as powerful as she was ambitious and gorgeous, she'd also been in a pretty bad way, and it wasn't very likely that she'd have lived long enough to get medical attention.

So, silly Lorcan, unable to allow this magnificent female to die right there in his arms, gave her some of his blood to allow her to rise again unscathed. Touching, right? Except, what the chivalrous moron hadn't realized was that the ethereal, wondrous creature was a witch. And when a witch gets partially turned by drinking vampire blood, what you get is a Blood Witch, a being full of unpredictable and dark magic. They're dangerous, powerful, and the idea of one makes absolutely no one happy.

As you can probably guess, I was that poor

damsel from the accident and after I was turned into a Blood Witch, I got turfed out of my coven and had to move to Haven Hollow to start over. True, the decision to come here had ended up being the best thing that ever happened to me. Not only had it gotten me out from under my insane mother's thumb, but I was now High Witch of my own coven, filled with people I respected. But I'd been pretty pissed about it at the time.

The vampires also weren't happy. Their leader, a vampire named Rupert (quite a silly vampire name, if you ask me), had ordered Lorcan to finish the job and turn me fully, thus removing the threat and my magic. It was either succumb to his wishes or we'd be killed. That hadn't gone so well for the vampires though, and had ended with Rupert dead, and all the vampires believing that I'd been fully turned. Yes, it grated on me, not being able to be acknowledged publicly as the High Witch I truly was, and having to keep to the night shift was getting old, but it was worth it if it kept everyone off our backs.

Though, it did leave me stranded with no back up in the face of a gaggle of giggling werewolves. Really, was peace worth this hell? I wasn't convinced.

After what felt like an eternity and a half,

but was probably closer to twenty minutes, one of the werewolves actually gathered up the courage to approach the counter. She was middle aged, gray just starting to creep in around the edges of her dark hair, and she smiled, but couldn't hold eye contact when she spoke to me. I forced a death grip on my temper.

Customer service, Wanda. You can't save them from themselves.

"Hello. I'm sorry to... well, to bother you... and please excuse me if I'm interrupting you from—"

"You're not."

"Oh, good." She blinked rapidly, clutching the edge of the counter. "Um, well, the reason we are here is that my, uh, my daughter is getting... well, married."

Of course, she was. I kept the thought off my face, and slapped on my best customer service smile, which I was fairly sure came off as a grimace because I was doing my best not to flash too many teeth. "Congratulations."

The woman beamed, almost visibly perking up. "Thank you. We wanted to get her something pretty for... well, for..." And then she dropped her face to the floor. "Her wedding night."

And then she blushed, and giggled this high-pitched, awful sound I hoped to never hear again. A middle-aged woman, mother of at least one and probably more, giggling like a teenager over the idea of sex. Goddess, have mercy on me.

She got a hold of herself finally and called to the gaggle of women behind her. "Bryony, come here, please."

The girl who stepped forward, separating herself from the rest of her pack, looked to be about nineteen. Tall, leggy, with her mother's dark hair. But she actually held her shoulders back instead of rounding them forward and stood with her hip cocked to one side. She didn't look like a bride, eager for her wedding. She appeared luke-warm at best, and that seemed strange. I mean, most brides I got in here appeared to be at least excited about getting married, but what did I know?

"We wanted something pretty," Bryony's mother continued. "And maybe spelled for fertility? I want grandpups. The sooner the better."

Bryony rolled her eyes at the same time that I did internally. It made me think there just might be hope for her, that is, if she could break away from the burden of her family.

"Of course, I can do that." I offered Bryony a smile, watching her with interest. "How about we look through my book of designs, and you can see if anything appeals to you? Or did you have something specific in mind?"

Bryony seemed a little surprised that I was directing my question towards her and not her mother. But the girl just shrugged, and let her mother and relatives crowd around the book while she hung back.

While four generations pored over my laminated book of designs, I beckoned Bryony over to the slightly raised platform at the back of the store. "I just need to get your measurements."

I got to work with my measuring tape, keeping half an ear out to the chatter over by the desk, and brushed off my unused and frankly shitty small-talk skills. "So, when's the big day?"

Bryony jolted, her forehead creasing as her brows pulled together. "Um... like, three weeks, I think."

She thought? That didn't sound promising. Weren't women supposed to be all excited and annoying about their upcoming nuptials, squealing and so on?

I ran my tape measure from her shoulder down to her hips and jotted a note in my book. "What's the groom like?"

"Mark?" Bryony shrugged, dragging the tape measure up and down with the movement. "He's fine, I guess."

It seemed I'd found someone even less interested in this conversation than I was. I decided not to bother, and just kept quiet for the rest of the session as I took the last few measurements so we could rejoin everyone at the counter.

Thus started the most annoying hour of my life. I'd dealt with brides before; some wonderful, some awful, and it was hard enough to get people to come to a decision about anything to do with a wedding. Now multiply that by thirty, with every aunt, cousin, sister, and grandmother voicing an opinion and the toddlers making sounds that would probably come to revisit me in my nightmares. Clothes weren't meant to be designed by committee.

And once they finally, *finally* decided on what Bryony's nightgown would look like, then they had to pick a fabric, lace, and what enchantments they wanted woven into the material. Everyone was talking over each other, and then apologizing for talking over each other, but continuing to do it anyway. There was a baby crying, a toddler trying to touch everything with fingers that looked like they'd survived World War III, and a migraine blooming to life in the middle of my forehead. A lesser woman might have snapped.

The only one who didn't seem heavily invested in making sure every single thing was absolutely perfect was, funnily enough, Bryony.

Finally, the design sketch was approved, the fabric and lace selected and the enchantments agreed upon, and everyone seemed happy. Most of all, me.

Bryony's mother signed the order and pushed it towards me. By force of will alone, I kept my attempt at a pleasant smile on my face. "Thank you, Mrs... Reid," I said, glancing down at the signed sheet. "With my current orders, it should take about two weeks to complete."

I'd pull Maverick in for it. He owed me after ditching me like he had. He was also better at delicate spell embroidery than I was, again, not that I would ever tell him as much over pain of death.

"I'll give you a call as soon as it's ready," I promised them, silently willing them to get out of my store as quickly as possible.

It took another few minutes of excited chattering, but eventually, the crowd milled out the door and down the street. Once they were out of sight, and I was reasonably sure they wouldn't be coming back, I let myself slump over the counter with a groan. I'd been smiling so long, my face actually hurt. How did Poppy manage it—always being so nice all the time? Were there smile strengthening exercises she did or something? I'd have to ask.

But for now, I figured I'd better file the paperwork as quickly as possible. And make several duplicates. If anything happened to their order, it might take them an entire day to try and remember what they'd picked out the first time, and that scared me in a way vampires, crazed witches, and vengeful faeries didn't.

Reid. The name seemed familiar, somehow. I didn't keep track of all the various werewolf families in the Hollow (because that would have been its own full-time job), and other than a polite acquaintance with Louisa Rutledge, I didn't really speak to them much. But the last name still nagged at me, and I wanted to place them.

Finally, I remembered. The Reid family. They'd been more recent residents to Haven Hollow, who'd bought the old, run down motel at the edge of town and fixed it up. The Blue Moon was still a motel, it was hardly a five-star affair, but at least driving past it these days, I didn't feel like I'd get fleas just by looking at it. Walking in? Well, that might be a different story.

The door opened, and I whirled around, terrified that the werewolf posse might have decided to change their order or something, but instead Maverick poked his head inside, giving me a scowl. Then he looked around the store, craning to see over some of the racks in the back.

"Are they gone?"

"Yes, you coward." I crossed my arms over my chest and glared at him. "How could you abandon me like that?"

He shrugged, completely unashamed, and lifted one of the paper cups he was carrying. "So, does that mean you don't want the coffee I brought you? If not, I'm happy to drink it—freaking thing cost me almost five bucks."

My smile had way too many teeth in it to be considered friendly. "Hand it over, cheapskate, and I might consider not hexing you bald."

He rolled his eyes at the threat, but handed over the delicious, steaming cup of heaven. After a few sips, even the giggle-induced migraine pounding in my skull started to ebb away.

Maverick twitched my sketchpad toward him, looking over the design I'd worked out with the Reids. He grunted and took a drink from his own coffee.

"Looks simple enough."

"The hardest part was figuring out what they wanted." I slumped back against the counter, trying to manually work the tension out of my back and shoulders. Where was my ridiculously hot vampire husband when I needed a massage, anyway? Honestly.

"To spell with it. I'm closing for the night,"

I announced.

"More than fine by me," my useless employee responded.

I strode over and flipped the sign on the door, locking it with a familiar motion. Maverick, meanwhile, seemed content to continue paging through my sketches, and though my fingers itched to snatch it away from him, I didn't. We were making progress, but things were still touchy between us sometimes. Being part of a coven, a full member at that, was something Maverick never would have thought could happen for him. Magic tended to favor women, and witches saw the occasional warlock that cropped up as somewhere between unfortunate and dangerous, depending.

Maverick was in something of a precarious position. Not only was he a warlock, but he had more power than most witches, which was almost unheard of. Add in the fact that he'd been blooded by a vampire war criminal on orders of my mother (who had wanted him turned to strip him of his magic and remove the stain of his birth from our former coven), and his power had become a dark, dangerous thing. He'd become a Blood Warlock and though there were ways of changing him back to the warlock he'd been previously, he had no interest in attempting it. I thought he actually embraced this new side of him, because it made him more an outsider than he already was. If he was discovered, no witch would rest until he was fully turned. Or burned at the stake. Maybe Maverick took some sort of perverse pride in that? I wasn't sure. But, whatever his reason, he didn't want to be returned to the way he used to be.

No one in the Scapegrace coven of Haven Hollow would ever rat him out, of course. But it felt like he thought his place in the coven might be yanked away from him at any second. So, baby steps.

"Do you have plans tonight?" I asked as I made my way back to the counter, tidying a shelf and straightening a hanger as I passed them.

"Why, are you trying to ask me out?"

I frowned at him. "You know I would never ask you out. I was just asking... well, to ask."

Maverick looked up, blinking, as though the attempt at small talk had confused him. His dark hair swung loose just below his shoulders, finally growing back out after he'd first had it cut in the attack that turned him into a Blood Warlock, and then again to infiltrate a group of vampires.

"Well," he said, slowly, pausing to take a sip of his coffee. Maverick was trying, too, it seemed. "I thought I'd go back to the coven house to tuck Sybil in. Then, I'll probably wait around for the inevitable call from Taliyah to help her out with a bunch of drunk werewolves." He jerked his chin towards the door. "I heard the group talking about a bachelor party going on tonight at the Half-Moon."

"Fun." I was a little surprised about the bedtime comment. Maverick had never struck me as the paternal type. When Sybil had first been 'born', he'd seemed entirely disinterested in her and had basically vanished into the horizon in a truly epic sulk.

But, once he'd figured out that I wasn't planning to lay claim to the girl and keep her from him, he'd done an almost entire about face. Since we couldn't exactly announce to the world that Sybil was the result of my and Maverick's blood magic reacting in an explosive event, and since Sybil was a shapeshifter who could appear as any woman she liked, but had chosen the form of a young witch of fourteen or fifteen, people would add the years and realize that I couldn't be her mother. The Crescent Circle coven had been a viper's den, but someone would have noticed if I'd gotten pregnant and given birth while there.

So, the official story was that Sybil was the result of a one night stand that Maverick had had years ago, and he'd only just found out about her. Truly, he'd embraced the role of Sybil's father with an eagerness that I hadn't really expected. He'd never talked about kids much before and I'd figured that, like me, he couldn't be bothered with them.

Or maybe fatherhood was just one more thing that Maverick assumed he'd never get to be or have, and so he'd latched onto it with the desperation of a man in the desert being offered a glass of water.

"Well, have fun wrangling the drunken werewolves," I told him, tugging my sketchbook back towards me. "Tomorrow, you can help me start thinking up fertility charms."

"Joy," he said, voice dry as he tossed his empty cup into the trash and breathed out a hearty sigh.

Chapter Two

In a town other than Haven Hollow, being forced to live by vampire hours would be tedious at best, and terrible at worst.

Fortunately for me, since its population was at least half made up of supernatural creatures of various flavors, Haven Hollow didn't suffer from the same restrictions as other small towns might, where the sidewalks rolled up the second the sun went down.

I wouldn't call the night life in the Hollow thriving by any stretch of the imagination—not like say, Las Vegas or New York, but there were certainly enough stores and attractions opened that I wasn't likely to wreak havoc out of sheer boredom. Lucky for them.

After closing up my shop and at least doing

a token amount of tidying so that Maverick didn't revolt in the morning, I headed to the Royal Theater, where Lorcan had invited me for date night to watch a late movie.

Just two blocks from Main Street, the Royal was like a place out of time. It reminded me of years gone by before movies had sound or color—it reminded me of the good ol' days. And at 142 years, I definitely had lived through many good ol' days. Everything at the theater was a little glitzy, and a little old fashioned, without crossing the line into tacky territory, and with that much gilt and red velvet, that was darn near a magic trick on its own.

There were statues out front, reclining on either side of the entrance doors. They looked like a cross between golden lions and Foo dogs from outside a temple. Raised up on stone platforms, they faced forward, heads alert even as they were lying down. As I passed them, I ran my fingers over the curls of one of their manes and felt a deep-down spark of old magic.

That made me pause a step.

Whatever enchantment was there, and there certainly was one, owing to that little zap I'd just received, it was old and faded. I wasn't even sure it would work anymore. But someone had clearly designed the statues for a purpose, even if I couldn't tell what that purpose was any longer.

I gave the guardian one last pat and stepped through the huge glass doors into the theater lobby. My heels sank into the plush carpet as I walked past the ticket booth towards the overstuffed couches over to one side of the lobby. The smell of fresh, buttery popcorn had my stomach growling and my mouth watering, and just listening to the soft *paf* of it sizzling away in the old-fashioned popper behind the snack counter made me smile. One good thing about dating a vampire was that I never had to share my food.

It was late for a normal theater to still be open, but at the Royal, they still had at least two showings before they closed around three or four in the morning. Assuming they sold any tickets, of course. There were only a few people in the building that didn't work there as far as I could see; two couples at the snack counter, picking out their treats. It meant that I got one of the plush couches in the lobby to myself, and I settled in to wait for Lorcan.

I was a little surprised he wasn't already here waiting for me, to be honest. Of the two of us, Lorcan certainly had mastered the whole being on time business better than I had (but, hey, it took time to look this good). I figured it was his late night at the office. Lorcan owned and operated Haven Hollow's only dental office, and he claimed he offered later hours for the convenience of his clients, but really it was the fact that he'd turn into a charcoal briquette if he set foot outside during the day. Not a good look.

I checked my phone, but I didn't have any texts or messages waiting, so I settled back into the plush cradle of the velvet couch, and busied myself with thinking about just how I was going to enchant Bryony Reid's nightgown.

That was, after all, what set Wanda's Witchery apart from other clothing stores. I didn't just design the clothing and make it, I wove spells into the fabric, painted them with potions and enchantments until it was soaked into the very fibers. If someone wanted a cocktail dress that would not only make them look amazing, but would actually make them look more graceful and confident, they came to me. Or maybe someone wanted to get into better shape—then they could get athletic wear that would make them feel energized and motivated to go to the gym until they formed the habit for themselves. Or maybe they were after lingerie that showcased their best features and softened their flaws, turning them into a sensual goddess—in all cases, they came to me and my store.

Bryony would need something that would make her feel beautiful on her wedding night, confident. And, of course, there were also the fertility charms her family wanted worked into the fabric. Something subtle, but something that was powerful enough to ensure she got the cubs she wanted.

Or did she want them? I had to admit, Bryony Reid was the most laid back, disinterested bride to have ever crossed my threshold. I'd dealt with a multitude of women getting married. Some had been excited, but pleasant. Others had been total nightmares, including one that had almost destroyed my business. But I'd never met one so uninterested in what was supposed to be the happiest day of her life (another facet to weddings that, in my mind, was just ridiculous).

Well, it wasn't any of my business. Werewolves were odd creatures, and they didn't tend to get along well with witches. But, then again, not many other supernatural creatures did. But, going back to my point, werewolf men thought women should be soft spoken caregivers, eager to raise the next generation of pups and nothing else—so no wonder they didn't approve of a witch's matriarchal society. More power to the women who enjoyed that, but it felt like indoctrination and brainwashing from a young age to me.

My backside was getting stiff, and I shifted

a bit and glanced at my phone, shocked at how late it was getting. There still wasn't any word from Lorcan, even though he was significantly late by this point. And that wasn't like him. Unless perhaps he'd forgotten about our movie date?

I crossed my legs, one foot bobbing furiously in the air as the minutes crept by. The movie we were supposed to watch had already started, and unless Lorcan showed up soon, we were going to miss the last showing of the night. The smell of popcorn and salt hovered in the air, taunting me.

Where the spell was he? No word, no call? He thought he could just leave me sitting there, like a fool? I didn't care if he'd accidentally forgotten! No one stood up Wanda Depraysie!

He had no excuse... unless there was some kind of emergency.

That made me pause, my foot in mid bob. What if there had been an emergency? What if something had happened to him? But then, as soon as that thought crossed my mind, I pretty much rejected it. Lorcan was a vampire, and not a particularly young one. He'd survived for centuries already, and that meant he was powerful. Very powerful. Not to mention the fact that the Hollow was supposed to be a safe, supernatural friendly zone. That was the point of them, after all, a place for paranormals to be able to live in peace next to their human neighbors. But in recent months, the Hollow had felt anything but safe.

The point was, Lorcan was incredibly difficult to harm, and even harder to kill. But that didn't mean either was impossible.

What if something had happened to him? If he'd gone and gotten himself killed, I'd murder him. Twice.

I'd sent him a couple of texts by this point, and even called once, but the call had gone directly to voicemail. I'd worked myself up to an uncomfortable pitch between anger and worry, and I'd started debating whether I should stay right where I was—just in case he showed up. Or was it better to head home and see if he was there? I was spared the need to decide, when I finally, *finally* got a response.

Sorry, Sweetling, the text read. *Something urgent came up. I can't make it tonight.*

Well, at least he wasn't dead. Or at least, not any more dead than when he'd left the house that evening. I should have been absolutely furious, and I was, but mostly I was baffled. Men did not leave me cooling my heels for an hour, and especially not Lorcan. He'd been chasing after me since the day we'd met, and suddenly I was getting stood up with a lame text explanation? Was Lorcan's desire for me finally cooling? Had we been together long enough now that he was less enthralled with me? Was this what women meant when they said something about the uselessness of marrying a cow if you could get milk from the grocery store?

I wasn't sure, but I was damned annoyed, all the same.

I, being extremely magnanimous, decided I'd wait until I saw him and heard his excuse before I hexed him with boils, or perhaps I'd cause all his teeth to fall out. Maybe he'd had to run into a burning building to save some orphans, or something. Though, he could have called once he beat the flames out, so, even then, it wasn't a perfect excuse.

I certainly didn't have any interest in watching a movie on my own, and I'd sat there alone long enough that I didn't want to be there any longer, so I grabbed my purse (a Louis Vuitton because... of course) and headed for the door, my head high and my spine as straight as a broomstick. Just let any of those little high school workers try and judge me. And thank the goddess that little rat Hellcat hadn't been anywhere near to witness my shame. I'd never hear the end of it.

I headed back to Lorcan's place, where I spent most of my nights when I wasn't at the coven house. I hadn't set foot in the little duplex across the graveyard from Poppy's place that had been my first home in Haven Hollow in months. I figured I should probably make a stop in at some point, just to make sure Libby the zombie was still up and lurching around.

I'd accidentally raised Libby from the dead when I'd first come to the Hollow and hadn't really had any idea how to control my Blood magic. New in town, and suddenly responsible for a housewife from the nineteen fifties who was a tried-and-true home maker, and fairly aggressive about it at that, life hadn't been exactly easy. At least with Poppy's help, I'd managed to keep Libby from rotting. Libby pretty much kept to herself these days, and I did feel a little bit sad at the fact that since Darla had moved into Cain Morgan's house, Libby was probably feeling a bit lonely lately.

Darla, the flapper ghost I'd managed to accidentally bring back to life, had also been my problem early on. But now she was working as a medium these days, and was currently on long term assignment channeling the late Police Chief Cain Morgan for his sister, the current Police Chief, Taliyah Morgan, so I figured that made her Taliyah's responsibility. And thank Hecuba for that.

So now I just had Sybil. At least my ability

to bring people to life or back to life was slowing its roll, because it would be damned awkward if people started noticing how the dead were becoming live again.

I pulled into the driveway a few minutes later, after speeding heavily. My near-death car accident hadn't really taught me anything. Besides, after being blooded by both Lorcan and the vampire terrorist who'd tried to murder Maverick, Janeth, I'd found myself a bit stronger, and a bit faster, and a great deal harder to injure. The pointed little tips of my teeth and the enhanced senses weren't bad, either. Though I could have done without the fact that blood actually smelled rather appetizing these days, as opposed to pennies and raw hamburger like it had for my entire life.

Honestly, waiting for Lorcan to get home wasn't any better than it had been waiting for him at the theater, though it was more private. In the house, there was no one to see me pace, or stare dramatically out the window, and then storm off, mad at myself for acting like the stupid wife in every made for TV drama ever made. Luckily, Hellcat had opted to live in the Coven house rather than stay with me at Lorcan's. And that was just as well, because the two of us couldn't stand one another. So, now he was able to bother any and everyone in the coven, and that suited me just fine. Trying to keep my thoughts occupied, I walked into the kitchen and reheated some food from the fridge while pouring myself a glass of wine. Then I seriously considered taking a bubble bath. Date night might be off, but that didn't mean my evening was ruined.

I was starting to get worried again as the hours rolled by and the sunrise crept closer and closer. What if Lorcan wasn't planning to make it home and had to spend the day in the coffin in the back of Marty's hearse? That meant I wouldn't see him until sunset again and that idea rattled around my head like a stray bomb.

When I finally heard the rattle of the keys in the door, I didn't fly into the front hall like some woman welcoming her sailor back from the sea. Instead, I took a deliberate sip of my wine, schooled my face into a neutral mask, and waited for the man to come to me.

Lorcan finally appeared in the kitchen, his surprisingly loud footsteps announcing his arrival. He shuffled in, still in his scrubs with a jacket he didn't need thrown over his shoulder. He looked tired, and worn, with dark circles under his beautiful green eyes, and his hair looked like he'd run his hand through it so many times, it had eventually given up and now just stood up in blond spikes.

I felt a tiny twinge of compassion in my heart, but ruthlessly stomped it out. Emergency or not, I had been stood up, and I deserved a proper grovel. Or, at least, an 'I'm sorry' ice cream cone from Stomper's Creamery.

"Hello, Sweetling," Lorcan said blearily, heading my way. "Sorry about tonight. Got held up at work. I'll make it up to you."

Lorcan had been turned into a vampire in his early forties, leaving him with only a few faint lines at the corner of his eyes for all eternity. He was dapper, and dashing, but for the first time I'd ever known him, he actually looked his age. There were lines creasing his brow, and stress pulling his cheeks tight. His eyes were blood-shot, which I hadn't even thought was possible. It must have really been a night.

And then he dropped an absent kiss on the crown of my head like I was a toddler and shuffled through the kitchen towards the bedroom.

What the what? I thought to myself as I whirled around and faced his retreating back.

Perhaps I could let him off the hook. Just for the night. He could grovel once he'd rested and eaten. And he would, by goddess, be making it up to me.

I nodded to myself, then paused, my nose wrinkling up.

With my enhanced vampire senses, I picked

up on smells a lot more than the average person could—think bloodhound but like half as good. Normally, when Lorcan came home from the clinic, he tended to smell of antiseptic, mint, and sometimes soap or the latex from his gloves. Normal things that he might pick up from any medical office.

So, why was it that I'd caught the hint of sweet vanilla when he'd bent down to kiss my head?

Chapter Three

As I suspected, Lorcan gave me a proper apology the next evening when he woke up, and he made sure to get off work a bit early so we could catch the movie while it was still in the theater.

After smelling that vanilla scent on him the night before, I was a bit cool with him, doing everything in my power not to blow my lid. Because it could simply be a case of a little, old lady giving him a hug after he'd successfully done whatever dentists do to dentures. The vanilla scent didn't have to mean that Lorcan was fooling around on me.

At least, that's what I kept telling myself and by now, I mostly believed it. After another conversation with myself, I'd pretty much decided to let it go, because I didn't want to be *that* woman—the kind who flew off the handle in a jealous rage for no apparent reason. And it did help that, a few nights later, Lorcan handed me his credit card and suggested I go into Portland on a fabric shopping trip. I was out the door so fast, I left a witch-shaped dust cloud in my wake.

Sure, I could get fabrics online and delivered to my door. But there was nothing like getting to pour through the racks of carefully rolled bolts of cloth. To feel the weave under my fingertips and see the colors in person and breathe in that scent. I was pleased just thinking about it on the drive there.

I left basically the instant the sun set. The days might have been getting shorter again, but I'd still only have a couple hours to shop my little heart out. I broke half a dozen laws speeding all the way into Portland, and soon enough I was blissfully pawing through the first, and best, of the fabric stores there. There were so many beautiful things to choose from; gorgeous cloth in every shade and texture, not to mention thread and notions. It was enough to make my black little heart pitter patter excitedly.

While I did take commissions when someone had a specific clothing item they wanted, a lot of the time I just made what I thought people would want to stock the store. A great deal of it was handmade, because that was the easiest way to set the spells and charms into the fabric —when something hadn't yet had a life of its own and, consequently, absorbed the energy from that life. I had been known to buy a few higher end articles of clothing from consignment shops on occasion though—when people were a little more budget conscious.

I was working my way down one aisle of the fabric store when I spotted it. The most luscious, wine-red satin I'd ever seen in my life. It was absolutely gorgeous, with a subtle sheen, a tight weave, and it spilled over my fingers like cool water.

Forget making something for my store, I was going to fashion something for myself with the luscious fabric. I had no idea what, but whatever it was, it was going to be amazing. My mouth was watering just thinking about it.

Pleased with myself, and with a hefty charge on Lorcan's credit card, I dropped my carefully wrapped prize in the trunk of my car and thought about getting something to eat. Real vampires didn't eat food, but I still had to. Blood couldn't sustain me, no matter how good it smelled these days. And besides, no one knew I was in Portland. If I was careful, I was sure it would be fine.

Luckily for me, there was a small pub not far from where I was parked. It looked like the kind of place students would congregate: not terribly fancy, but good food, and relatively unknown. I might be about a hundred and twenty-two years older than the usual clientele, but they certainly wouldn't know it.

With thoughts of a chicken Caesar wrap putting a bit of speed into my step, I was tempted to just power walk into the couple having a rather intense discussion right in front of the restaurant. I didn't have much patience on the best of days for people getting in my way, but when I was hangry, everyone beware. I was just winding up to tell them to take it elsewhere, when the girl turned far enough that I could see her profile when she tucked her hair back behind her ear.

"Bryony," I said, surprised. I hadn't expected to see her here—so far from her family.

She jumped, and rounded on me, her eyes wide. The man with her reached out and hesitated, like he was going to put his arm between us to keep me from reaching her—like he thought I was going to attack her or something. Clearly, he must have caught on to the fact that I was a witch—or maybe he'd heard I was a vampire.

I gave him a look that promised he'd regret

it if he tried to touch me, and he was smart enough to shrink back out of my way. I didn't know who he was, but I could tell by smell alone that he wasn't a werewolf, so he couldn't be Bryony's groom to be. He was definitely a supernatural, though. There was a glamour draped over him, hiding his true features, leaving him dark-haired, dark eyed, and remarkably human looking. Draping oneself in a human guise wasn't unusual, especially among supernaturals who couldn't pass for human—this way they could blend in better.

Bryony smiled at me, but it was a sickly thing. "Oh, hello. Wanda, was it? I wasn't expecting to see you here."

She was nervous, her eyes wide and darting. It was an odd change from the girl who'd been completely unimpressed by everything in my store, but then, werewolves tended to be a lot more retiring when they didn't have their pack around.

"Same." I glanced at the young man still hovering awkwardly by the pub windows, but then turned back to Bryony. "Anyway, your order is ready, and you can pick it up whenever you're available."

The nightgown had been easy enough, the design hadn't been an elaborate one. And with Maverick helping me with the enchantments, we'd managed to wrap it up fast. I'd wanted a bit of extra time, to make sure everything was how she wanted it, since the wedding was coming up fast. Running into Bryony was a stroke of luck, since it meant I didn't have to put a phone call to the lady werewolf mafia. Hopefully she'd pick it up alone, and I wouldn't have to deal with the hordes descending on my store again.

And given the fact that I hadn't actually ordered anything from the restaurant, my cover wasn't completely blown. Still, I looked up at the sign which clearly proclaimed itself to be a deli, and frowned.

"Oh, I thought this was a shoe store—silly me," I continued with an embarrassed shrug.

Bryony smiled, and it was faker than a twenty-dollar Prada bag. "That's great you finished it. Thank you so much. I'll be in to get it tomorrow." Then she tossed a nervous look at the guy she'd been talking to and folded her arms across her midriff. "I'm just confirming some stuff with the restaurant. We're hiring some servers for the reception to pass around appetizers and drinks."

Weddings ranked about a zero on the list of things I cared about, a stranger's wedding even lower. And there was a wrap calling my name inside the pub, so I just smiled absently as I tried to figure out where I could hide until Bryony left so I could make sure the coast was clear to order my food. "Okay. I'll see you later, then."

The girl's shoulders relaxed as I walked by, but she couldn't seem to meet my eyes, keeping her gaze firmly on the sidewalk. I fought not to sigh. It was such a pity. I'd thought she had a bit of a back bone, at least.

***

By the time I walked back out of the restaurant, no longer hungry and cranky, the pair was long gone, so at least I got to avoid another awkward conversation. I was halfway back to the car when my phone rang with Lorcan's ringtone.

"Sweetling," he said, something odd in his tone. "Where are you?"

"Still in Portland." I glanced around to make sure no cars were coming before crossing the street. "I'm almost back to my car, and then I'll be heading home. Why? Can you smell your credit card burning from there?"

He laughed, a low, rich chuckle that had my belly tightening. "I actually was wondering if you could do me a little favor."

"Every day I tolerate you is a favor, Rowe."

I paused as he chuckled once more. "But I might be persuaded. What's the favor?" I leaned against my car, not bothering to unlock it.

Across the line, I heard fabric rustle. Lorcan kept his voice quiet, like he didn't want to be overheard. "I have an order that needs picking up. I could make the drive tomorrow, but since you're already there, I thought you might grant me a boon."

Most of the stores were already closed, so there was no way he'd be able to get whatever it was if I didn't pick it up for him. And since the vampire had just indulged my expensive shopping spree, I figured I could pick up whatever it was for him. I gave a dramatic sigh for appearances, though. "I suppose."

"Thank you, Sweetling. I'll see you when you're home." He rattled off the store I needed to go to. And then he hung up, before I could say goodbye. And, I noticed with interest, that he hadn't bothered with any of the little lovey sentiments he usually ended our calls with. There was no mention of my lady bits and how much he was looking forward to reuniting with them, no mention of the nicknames he called me when it was just the two of us (nicknames I absolutely refuse to list, because they're *that* mortifying). Nothing at all.

I stared at the phone, blinking in shock for a

few seconds.

Suddenly in a sour mood, I jerked my car door open, ready to have the rest of the night over with.

***

I was never going to forgive him for this.

How could he? How dare he? We were so over. Divorced. Done. Kaput. Over.

He could have his blood back, but I was keeping the car.

I stood in line for the customer service desk in the most obnoxious big box store I'd ever seen. The fluorescents were giving me a headache, and the bland music echoing through the tinny PA system was enough to induce rage in my soul. What could Lorcan even want from such a place?

We shuffled forward another step, and I had to resist the urge to hex everyone in the building. It probably wouldn't have done much good, anyway. I'd met a zombie that was livelier than the staff here. Or the customers, for that matter.

With every second I was forced to wait, my temper crept a little hotter, like the red line in a thermometer. If I didn't reach the cashier soon, I was going to erupt. Finally, it was my turn to talk to the dead-eyed teenager who was chewing gum in an obnoxious, open-mouthed way that reminded me of a cow chewing its cud.

"I have an order for pick up under the name: Lorcan Rowe."

The teenager gave an enormous sigh, like my asking her to do her job was the greatest inconvenience ever suffered by mankind.

My fists slowly clenched.

She took an inordinately long time searching the shelves behind the register, pawing through the stacks of items put aside there. When she finally turned back around, I almost shrieked at what she had in her hands.

Lorcan had put me through this indignity for a phone charge cable? A thing we already had over a dozen of? A thing he could have bought in any number of stores right in Haven Hollow? A thing he could HAVE ORDERED FROM AMAZON?!

My nails dug into my palms hard enough that I was going to have permanent little crescent divots in my skin.

"You're lucky it's here," the cashier told me, in a voice that was completely without inflection, but still managed to sound extremely nasal. "The order just came in. You're supposed to wait until we email you."

I told myself to count to five, before turning back with a baring of teeth that only a drunk or an idiot would call a smile. "Oh? Well, so sorry to have troubled you," I said in a sickeningly sweet voice that I may or may not have copied from Poppy. Though her version was less sarcastic certainly.

As I tapped Lorcan's card to pay for the stupid thing, I glanced up at the computer screen where the order was still displayed. The time ordered was less than ten minutes ago. That meant, Lorcan would've ordered it after he hung up the phone with me. So, he hadn't had an order waiting at all. He'd made the order specifically so I'd have something to pick up. But why?

Confused and a little frustrated, I took the bag with the charger and stormed out of the store. The automatic doors came within inches of being hexed off their tracks, but luckily for them, they opened in time.

Why would Lorcan order something so stupid? Just to delay me in coming home? Why would it matter what time I got back to the house? Or was he trying to stall me from getting back to Haven Hollow? Either way, he was trying to delay me and I wanted to know why.

Maybe I was thinking about it too hard. It was possible the silly man had just forgotten to ever put the order in and then hearing I was in Portland, decided to put it in right then. But why special order something so easily found anywhere else? It made no blasted sense, and I didn't like things that made no blasted sense.

Chapter Four

I barricaded myself behind the counter at Wanda's Witchery and tried to figure out what the spell was up with Lorcan.

He was trying to keep me from getting home, but why? Did he have some sort of surprise planned? If he had a surprise party for me, I was really going to kill him. But there wasn't a reason to have a party in the first place.

It wasn't our anniversary, no matter which way you looked at it. Not an anniversary commemorating the moment we were married, not one commemorating the moment we'd started dating, not even the day he gave me his blood to keep me from dying. It wasn't my birthday, and quite frankly, a surprise party for a witch was liable to end up with someone hexed. And it wasn't his birthday. It wasn't Yule, his dog's, birthday either.

So, what in the hell was going on with him lately? Staying out late—missing our date, trying to keep me out of town, being tired and stressed, and downright taciturn for the last week. Usually, I couldn't stop Lorcan's mouth with all the magic in the world, and suddenly it was nothing but exhausted silences and a few clipped words.

At the rate he was going, I was going to have to lock him in a coffin and sit on it until he agreed to spill what was going on with him. I wasn't a patient witch to begin with, and all of this was testing my last nerves.

A piercing giggle had me gritting my teeth so hard, they squeaked.

It certainly wasn't helping that I'd been invaded by the female half of the Reid clan yet again.

I'd really thought that by telling Bryony specifically to come and pick up her order, that I might be able to spare myself a second invasion of the time snatchers. Watching grown women giggle over a bit of white silk and lace was something no one needed to be subjected to. Especially a woman whose husband was acting so weird, we actually hadn't even had sex in days.

The one saving grace was at least they'd showed up when Maverick was still here, and this time, he didn't get the opportunity to ditch me. One of the mid-teen girls of the family had latched onto his arm and was in the process of actually fluttering her eyelashes at him, which was both hilarious and slightly repulsive.

Though, the look on Maverick's face—watching him trying to keep his customer service smile in place while looking like he was trying not to laugh and/ or vomit was almost worth the assault on my eardrums.

I didn't know why I'd bothered packaging the nightgown up so carefully in tissue paper and a garment box. The instant I'd brought it out, the crowd had opened it right back up again, and pulled it out, insisting that Bryony hold it up and let them ooh and ah over it, which at least was mildly gratifying.

At least they didn't demand she put it on and parade around. It wasn't that kind of store.

Not that there was anything particularly scandalous about the thing—but it was a nightgown. And a wedding negligee at that. I might not have known much about weddings, but I was pretty sure the idea was for only your husband to see you in it.

With the full weight of four generations of peer pressure on her, Bryony did pick up the nightgown and held the straps up to her shoulders so the silk fabric spilled down over her body. It might not have been the most intricate design I'd ever come up with, but it was elegant and classic in its simplicity. The silk was ivory, with a gathered bodice and a waistline that sat just under the bust, so the creamy fabric spilled almost straight to the floor. It was designed so that, when the wearer moved, the fabric would cling to the hips or the thighs, sensual in what it hinted at, rather than something more risqué, like peekaboo panels or the like.

Trimmed with delicate ivory lace, and a hint of white-on-white embroidery that held the enchantments they'd asked for, I had to admit, it was a lovely piece. While the others all chattered about how beautiful it was, Bryony was silent. She lifted a hand to stroke the smooth, cool fabric where it lay against her stomach, and then let her arm drop. I couldn't quite place the expression she was wearing, and I almost asked if there was something wrong with the nightgown.

Then, at a lull in the noise, she said very quietly, "It's beautiful."

The horde converged on her then, smiling, crying, congratulating her. Only Bryony was still, looking down at the ivory silk. She was silent, just brushing the tips of her fingers back and forth across the slippery fabric.

Maverick, who'd managed to deftly extract himself from his admirer, retreated behind the counter with me. I smirked at him, but he pretended not to see it.

Mrs. Reid, who had gushed "Oh, please, call me Thea," when I'd first brought the night gown out, was now openly sobbing—taking in heaving, snotty gulps of air. I hoped like spell she didn't touch anything in the store because 'snot spelled' didn't need to be part of my repertoire. Her whole body was quivering with the force of her breathing.

"I'm going to be a grandmother," she cried, and blew her nose with a distressingly wet sound.

That seemed a little over the top. Yes, the nightgown was spelled to encourage fertility, but it wasn't like Bryony was going to get knocked up the second she put it on. Besides, I didn't understand why Thea was so excited about having grandchildren when some of the girls in the throng seemed to be Bryony's sisters and with the toddlers running around, I figured they belonged to some of the younger women.

While the rest of the mob surrounded Bryony, Thea came over to the counter to cry at me for some reason. "It's so perfect." She blew her nose again, and I not so subtly pushed a bottle of hand sanitizer closer to her on the counter.

Thea didn't notice. "It's all going to be so perfect. We're having the ceremony outside on the full moon, in the field next to the motel. And everyone in the family is helping to make the meal. Right at moonrise—that's when they'll take their vows."

I couldn't think of a tactful way to tell her that it was literally impossible for me to care less, and there was also the chance that they might become repeat customers, so I just plastered on the customer service smile it had taken me months to learn, and nodded.

"Oh!" Thea looked between Maverick and me, her face glowing, and not just from blowing her nose too much. "You should come, both of you! It's going to be wonderful, I'm sure you'll have a great time, and the more the merrier! It's going to be quite the to-do."

Maverick, probably sensing that I was one more piercing giggle away from telling them I'd rather glue my nostrils together than go, stepped in and used the charm he apparently had when he wasn't dealing with family.

"That sounds amazing, Thea, and thank you so very much for inviting us and I would love to come. It sounds like you've put a lot of effort into planning everything, so it all goes off just right."

Thea straightened up, her face shining with pride. "Yes, we have. Oh, but there's still so much to do." Then she turned to the rest of the pack. "Come on ladies, we need to get to our next stop."

And thank the goddess for that.

It took another ten minutes for them all to herd out, but eventually, they were gone and I could breathe a little easier, even as I wondered if I should start disinfecting the place. The shop was suddenly so silent that I could almost hear it ringing. It was blissful.

I shoved at Maverick's shoulders, pushing him out from behind the counter. "Quick, lock the door. Before they decide to come back."

Once the store was locked up, and the sign set to closed, I let myself slump back against the counter. My neck ached, and there was a knot wedged up underneath my shoulder blade, but it was finally done. Another satisfied customer. Or fifty.

I reached back as far as I could and dug my thumb into the muscle of my shoulder, trying to relieve the knot. "You're not really going to go to the wedding, are you?"

Maverick didn't leer, or offer to rub my shoulders for me, which was a sign of how far we'd come. Once upon a time, he would have taken any excuse he could get to touch me.

Taliyah was a good influence on him.

He shrugged. "I might as well. A moonrise ceremony with a bunch of drunk, celebrating werewolves. Taliyah and I will probably get called in anyway, so we might as well get a drink and a meal out of it."

He actually had a point.

"And since they're your clients, you should go too."

I frowned, but then the more I thought about it, the more it started to appeal to me—simply because it would be a night out that gave me an excuse to dress myself up to the nines, and drink on someone else's tab. A bit of mental math confirmed that, yes, it was Lorcan's late night at the office, so he wouldn't be able to go with me, but why should I sit at home waiting for him, anyway? I'd wear a killer dress and heels, and maybe I'd send him a picture that made him regret having to work.

The thought made me falter. I still didn't know what was up with Lorcan and his weird behavior lately, and I wasn't sure how to bring it up without sounding like I was jealous or something equally offputting. In general, I didn't do emotions. I hadn't been raised to react well to them and even though I was learning the Grinch's lesson and my heart had grown at least two times since I'd moved to Haven Hollow, I still wasn't ready to play the part of jealous wife. Not only that, but I was also the High Witch of a coven, and I was accustomed to a certain level of attentiveness. Perhaps that's all this was—that my expectations were up at the top of Mount Everest, and Lorcan was failing to live up to them lately.

"Everything all right?" Maverick asked, his tone wary.

Well, spell, it must have been obvious that everything wasn't alright if even my useless cousin was noticing. It was almost sweet if you liked those Hallmarky sort of moments. But I'd have rather eaten live spiders than ever discuss my relationship problems with him. He'd never let me live it down.

So, I brushed him off. "It's nothing. Just thinking about what inventory I might need to restock."

It was pretty obvious that Maverick didn't buy it. But he'd also grown up in a coven, until he got kicked out for the dual sins of being powerful and a male, so he knew better than to press a witch to talk about something personal. That's how people got hexed.

I grabbed my bag from under the counter. "Now, let's get out of here. I don't know about you, but I need a drink after tonight."

Chapter Five

I had to hand it to the Reid pack; they did put on an excellent shindig.

The Blue Moon motel was close to the edge of town, with about thirty rooms and lots of parking. The field right next to it was enormous —big enough that the wedding wasn't occurring right next to the building. And there was a privacy screen of evergreen trees between the motel windows and the party.

Someone had strung large orb lights on poles, with dainty fairy lights woven between the branches of the pine trees along one side of the field. Once the moon rose, there would be plenty of light to see by, but the setup still allowed the shadows to keep everything soft and private.

It was a werewolf party, which meant there was a truly astonishing amount of food. The far table, set up like a buffet, was practically groaning under the number of trays and chaffer dishes sitting on it. I wasn't quite sure what I'd been expecting, maybe burgers and hot dogs, but a Fourth of July barbeque this definitely was not.

It was meat heavy, which I'd expected. But there was everything from meatballs in a tangy sweet sauce, to steaks, to salmon covered in a lemon and dill sauce. Whole roasted turkeys were arranged, ready to be carved. Right beside the turkeys was a lamb roast and next to that, there were ribs, and chicken wings, and a whole mess of sides. Everything from potato salad to cornbread, with a pity salad pushed to the corner as the only vegetables I could see, other than the cobs of corn done on the grill and piled high onto a tray.

People were milling around, as the meal was supposed to start right after the ceremony. Standing there, smelling the delicious scents, it was a little bit of torture, honestly. Fortunately, Thea Reid knew her guests, and that meant she knew hungry werewolves in a confined area drinking alcohol would probably end in fur flying, so there were also servers in white shirts and black slacks milling through the crowd, with trays of appetizers as well as glasses of wine.

I was in the process of eyeing a tray coming my way that had what looked like golden puffed sausage rolls, when I realized the server carrying the tray was the same man I'd seen with Bryony in Portland. He was still wearing his glamor, which was a little strange. The venue wasn't exposed to anyone who shouldn't have been there, and literally everyone who was present was a supernatural of one type or another. Point being, it wasn't like he had to hide.

Maybe he was a really strange looking species, and he didn't want to draw attention to himself or something. We'd been getting more and more of those since Fifi had taken over the real estate agency in town. Or maybe his glamour was part of his contract. If he'd been female, I would have thought he might be a hag trying to contain her aura of decay. I could see that making a serving job a lot more difficult.

I shrugged. What the waiter was or why he was covering himself up wasn't really any of my business. Unlike witches, who were proud of their power and wanted everyone to know it, some supernatural types were shy, or feared too much attention, even in a Hollow.

The waiter glanced around and then set his full tray down on a nearby table before ghosting off into the crowd. I frowned. That was odd.

Maybe he had to answer the call of nature? Or maybe he was going to help another server with something?

"Wine, ma'am?"

The waitress who approached me only came up to my chin. She had a mass of bright, copper colored curls and big green eyes. Not to mention, she smelled like apple blossoms and sun-baked grass. Fae of some type, most likely. But more importantly, she had a tray of glasses filled with wine, which made her my new favorite person.

I snagged a glass with a smile, and she hustled away while I took a sip.

"Aren't you supposed to save that to toast the happy couple?"

I turned just far enough to acknowledge Maverick, who was coming up behind me, and I exaggeratedly raised my glass before I took another sip. "I'm toasting them privately. May they live happily ever after in the moonlight, and have many fat babies."

Maverick rolled his eyes, but then Taliyah appeared beside him, and she gave me a nod of greeting, which I returned.

I rather liked Taliyah Morgan. And not just because she seemed capable of keeping my cousin's more obnoxious personality traits in check. I liked that she'd forged her own path and refused to let anyone guilt or shame her into something (aka an arranged marriage) that wasn't in her best interests.

Taliyah had been born Princess Olwen of the Winter court of faerie, but she'd lived almost half a century as a human, never knowing who or what she really was. Then her adoptive brother, Cain Morgan, had been murdered in the line of duty as Haven Hollow's Chief of Police, and Taliyah had come to find out what happened. And she'd taken his place as the new chief.

Then the seal on her identity had been broken early.

Suddenly, she had all kinds of power, and her body was changing, and everyone was telling her she needed to go back to Faerie and marry a man she'd never met and become Queen. Never mind her two adopted children, or her life that she'd worked hard for, nope never mind all that. Just dust it all away and do what some prophecy told her to.

Taliyah had told them all, quite succinctly, where to stick it, and had continued on serving and protecting the Hollow. Though, with a few new powers and a better understanding of exactly what was going on. There were some fairly serious political problems, and a great deal of fighting, but I would have done exactly the same thing, had I been in her place.

Truly, of all the women in Haven Hollow, I most identified with Taliyah. Yes, Poppy was my closest friend and I would destroy anyone who tried to hurt her (or her son), but Taliyah and I were cut from the same fabric. We could understand one another. If it weren't for the fact that she was fae and platinum blonde, she could have easily been born a witch—she was that strong.

Since there weren't any humans in the crowd, Taliyah hadn't bothered with the glamour that made her look human. So, instead of a shoulder-length, no nonsense bob of graying brownish hair, she had a waist-length fall of pure silver that was twisted into a simple updo. Her skin was flawless, the little lines at the corners of her eyes and mouth erased. The only part of Taliyah that never changed were those brilliant, ice blue eyes.

She was looking quite nice in a floaty dress of pale lilac. I sensed my cousin's hand in that, since Taliyah was more of a jeans and T-shirt kind of person when she was off duty. They looked good together, I had to admit. Relaxed in a way I rarely saw Maverick. Fortunate, I thought, since they were technically married.

I'd married them myself, in fact, and the spell had gone a bit deeper than even I had intended. Maverick had made the offer as a way for Taliyah to circumnavigate her betrothal of the Prince of Autumn, Reynard. Or as I'd met him, Fox Aspen. The relationship wasn't typical, and it was rare for a witch to marry, never mind a warlock. But it seemed to be working for them, and I was hardly in a position to judge.

Maverick gave me a glance and lifted his wine glass to take a sip. "Where's your bloodsucker?"

I covered my annoyance with a sip from my own glass. Rule one for witch socializing; never let them see when they get under your skin. "He's working tonight. He'll either join me when he finishes, or I'll meet him at home."

Assuming he showed up this time. I kept my face blank, not wanting to give anything away. Maverick had never liked Lorcan, partially because he'd had some weird crush on me for years, mostly because I was the only witch who'd ever been half-way decent to him. Thank goddess he was finally over that crush, or us being in a coven together again would have been very uncomfortable.

I glanced at my phone and frowned at the time. I'd thought the ceremony was supposed to have started a half an hour ago. The groom was already here, standing by the flower arch and the werewolf who was acting as the officiant was waiting too. A bunch of the groom's male relatives had gathered around, slapping his shoulder and hyping him up from the looks of things.

The groom didn't look like a man getting married. He looked like a man who'd been told he was getting his favorite body part amputated. His mood was certainly somber and to see him moping around, staring at the ground, you might think someone just died. He looked resigned, not particularly happy. His reaction reminded me of Bryony's sullen quiet on her first visit to the shop.

So, not a love match, then. Why even bother getting married? Goddess help me, but I did not understand this very strange institution.

If we were all going through with this farce, then I wished that they'd get a move on. According to one of the cousins I'd recognized from the female werewolf brigade, Bryony was just getting ready in one of the motel rooms. It was less than a hundred feet away, so there was no way she could get lost.

The crowd was getting restless. There was less happy laughter and more mumbling, people craning their heads around to look and see if there was any sign of the bride. Maverick and Taliyah were watching the younger male werewolves who had seemingly decided to start pre-drinking for the event with a kind of annoyed resignation on their faces. This was going to be one afterparty I was glad I wasn't going to have to clean up.

Honestly, I was thinking about ducking out. I'd only come because I didn't have anything better to do and I liked to dress up. But the shoes I'd thought were so pretty were starting to pinch, not to mention how the heels kept sinking into the grass. They had one job, to make my legs look incredible. Mission successful, but they weren't designed for walking on grass, and I was getting tired of aerating the lawn with every step. The only werewolves I had even a passing familiarity with had ducked out to go check on Bryony, so now was the perfect time to slip away without having to make an excuse.

I was just about to tell Maverick and Taliyah I was ducking out when the howls started.

At first, I thought it was just part of the ceremony. I'd never been to a werewolf wedding before, but howling seemed like a plausible thing to expect. But the werewolf guests didn't react like it was a good or expected thing. Almost in unison, every werewolf at the party turned toward the motel. Just their heads, swiveling like they'd all been jerked by a string. It might have been funny, if it weren't for the expressions on their faces.

"What's going on?" Taliyah was already reaching for her clutch, and I would have bet my favorite pair of heels that her badge and service weapon were stashed inside it.

"No idea," Maverick murmured, trying to use his ridiculous height to see what was going on.

The howling kept going, out of pitch, loud and almost desperate. I didn't understand whatever cue was going out to the werewolves present, but it was still making me uneasy. Gooseflesh crept down my arms, and the hair on the back of my neck prickled. What the spell was going on?

Thea Reid burst through the screen of evergreens; her red face twisted into a rictus as she sobbed. Her hair was disheveled, sagging out of its careful updo and down over one eye. The rest of the women who'd gone with her followed, looking almost as upset. There were a lot of tears and snot, and I didn't have a lot of experience, but it didn't look like they were happy crying about the big day.

A male werewolf with graying brown hair hurried forward, Bryony's father I assumed, and Thea threw herself into his arms, howling and sobbing. He gripped her arms, asking her something quietly but urgently. The crowd was getting anxious, people moving closer, trying to find out what was going on.

Thea sobbed something into her husband's chest, and he stiffened, before yanking her back by the shoulders. Free from the muffling of cloth and werewolf chest, it suddenly became really easy to hear just what Mrs. Reid was wailing.

"She's dead! She's dead! My little girl!"

I froze. The crowd erupted into shouts and snarls. The groom to be shouldered his way forward, demanding to know what was going on.

Thea Reid was a mess, and the relatives clustered around weren't any better. Ugly sobs and howls made it hard to understand just what she was saying at first, but her voice was getting louder and louder.

"Bryony's dead. She's dead!" Her words spiraled up into a howl of grief.

"Dead how?" Mr. Reid demanded. "Did someone attack her?"

Growls rippled through the crowd, and some of the people standing near me suddenly seemed to be sporting twice as many teeth as before. It was about to get ugly for whoever was responsible.

Mrs. Reid whipped her head back and forth, her hair lashing at her face. "No! She was just lying there on the bed, her hands crossed on her stomach. I thought she was sleeping, at first. She was even in her... nightgown."

The last word trailed off into a low, threatening snarl, and Mrs. Reid's eyes met mine through the crowd. Her teeth were bared, eyes shimmering gold like a cat in the dark.

What the spell was going on?

"You," she snarled, jabbing a finger at me. Gone was the subservient and shy woman in my shop. From the looks of it, she'd been replaced with a harpy. And as to that finger she was pointing in my direction, it was tipped in a long, hooking claw still painted a lovely mulberry shade. "You did this!" She screamed. "Witch! Your magic killed my little girl!"

I gaped at her, speechless. What in the world was she talking about?

Mrs. Reid surged forward, but others caught her, holding her back, though they looked uncertain about it.

I couldn't believe what I was hearing. "I didn't–"

Mrs. Reid snarled, a low ripping sound like a chainsaw chewing through solid wood. She lunged and managed to drag three people a step closer to me. "There wasn't a mark on her! Just that nightgown! You did this. *You did this*."

There were suddenly a lot of unfriendly faces pointed in my direction. Eyes that glowed gold or green in the rising moonlight. I saw shadows of hair sprouting, claws and fangs bared.

I was a Blood Witch, the leader of my own coven. That meant I was strong, but it didn't mean that I wanted to take on a werewolf bent on revenge, much less a whole pack of them. But it didn't look like I was going to get much of a chance to proclaim my innocence, either.

Everything hung on a knife's edge, with Mrs. Reid snarling and thrashing, and the people hanging onto her slowly loosening their grips. Something was going to give one way or another, and whatever that thing was, it was going to go very, very badly.

The first werewolf lunged forward, a young male with his blood up, and Taliyah blasted a line of frost across the assembled dancefloor.

Everyone jerked back instinctively, and Haven Hollow's chief of police stepped forward center stage. She lifted her badge up into the air and made eye contact with as many people as she could.

"Everyone, stop exactly where you're standing. We will get to the bottom of what's happened but no one is going to attack anyone. Do you all hear what I'm saying?"

It wasn't Taliyah's season, but you wouldn't have known that to look at her. She stood, totally unafraid, in front of a pack of werewolves out for revenge, and she didn't even flinch. Even in her heels and pretty dress, she looked every inch the Chief of Police.

When it was clear people were at least hesitating, she turned just far enough to speak to my cousin.

"Maverick, get her out of here."

Maverick hesitated, clearly torn.

She fixed him with a glare. "They aren't going to be rational if she's standing here and they think she's guilty. Go. Now. You can come back when she's safe."

That broke Maverick out of whatever dilemma he was having, and he actually grabbed my arm and half dragged, half escorted me away from the crowd. Normally, he would have gotten an earful for carting me around like baggage, magically and verbally, but I did want out of there before someone decided to take a bite out of me.

I couldn't believe Bryony was dead. Healthy werewolves aren't immortal, but they tended to be hard to kill. What would make a young woman just drop like that? And of course, trust werewolves to come scratching at my door for magic, and then turn around and try to bite.

The logical part of my mind understood that Mrs. Reid had just had a terrible shock, and was lashing out, looking for a target for her grief. But the less charitable parts of me were absolutely indignant. If I were going to kill someone, it wouldn't be a teenage werewolf. Furthermore, if I wanted someone dead—I would never have been stupid enough to get caught.

Not to mention there was no way the spells that Maverick and I had put on that nightgown could ever actually harm anyone.

Could they have?

That thought, along with Maverick's ridiculously long stride, made me stumble.

Because when Maverick and my magic came together, the effects were... dramatic.

But that was when our magic coming together was unexpected. If I dropped a potion on an enchantment he was doing, sure, we might make a living mannequin, but the nightgown had been so carefully laid out. We hadn't even worked our magic at the same time. There shouldn't have been anything in the spell that could even cause a headache, much less death.

So why was there a cold lump of dread settling into my stomach?

Chapter Six

Haven Hollow wasn't the kind of town that normally required round the clock policing.

It had its fair share of mundane crimes, as much as any small town would, but it was nothing like New York, or even Portland, with round the clock shifts of law enforcement. If someone needed help after hours, the humans could call the lone night dispatcher who would page out officers as needed. And the supernatural citizens? Well, we tended to police our own by way of the Council. Though, Taliyah coming into her power had blurred that line a bit, especially with Maverick acting as bounty hunter and magical back up for her.

It did mean that when I sat myself down in the chair across from Police Chief Morgan's desk at the station somewhere between way too late in the night and way too early the next morning, the place was dark and nearly deserted.

Taliyah had thrown a blazer over her dress, and she'd put on some running shoes at some point, but hadn't bothered to change out of her dress or let her hair down. She looked tired. Having to deal with three busloads of angry werewolves as well as process a crime scene wasn't exactly a picnic.

I still couldn't believe what was happening, but when Taliyah had asked to meet with me, I'd agreed. As soon as Maverick had gotten me back to my car, he'd turned and left without a word, on his way back to Taliyah. I'd gotten out of there, but I'd found myself just parked beside the graveyard by my old duplex, not really knowing where to go or what to think.

How could Bryony be dead? It didn't make any sense.

I wasn't sure I could add anything to the investigation, but for the moment, Taliyah was simply asking me for any help I might be able to give her, without involving any handcuffs. Not only that, but I didn't want to poke this particular polar bear, so I settled into my chair and made an effort to be helpful.

Taliyah downed her coffee like she was

throwing back a shot and made a face at the taste. "So. Walk me through the nightgown thing."

She'd offered me my own cup of coffee, but I'd only gotten the cup halfway to my mouth before the burnt bitter scent reached my nose and I put it back down again. I settled back into the uncomfortable visitor's chair, and crossed my legs, one foot bobbing in the air.

"I was commissioned by the Reid clan to make a nightgown for Bryony for her wedding night, and they wanted several enchantments worked into it."

Taliyah made a note. Or maybe she was just doodling, I couldn't tell from where I was sitting. "What enchantments?"

I fought back a sigh. "The usual—things to hide flaws and emphasize her best features. Enchantments to make her feel beautiful and confident. But also, fertility." I made a face. "Mrs. Reid wanted grandpups, stat."

Taliyah made another note, her face carefully blank, hiding whatever she was thinking. "And is there any reason you can think of why Mrs. Reid would accuse you of murdering her daughter?"

"No." I flung my hand up, exasperated. "I didn't even know the girl. I spoke to her all of three times, and just about the nightgown her family commissioned. I didn't kill her, and I had no reason to."

Never mind what rumors like that would do to my business. Who'd buy enchanted clothing if they thought there was a chance that instead of going to the gym, they might just drop dead?

"Is there any... other reason?" Taliyah tapped her pen against her desk, her brow furrowed.

"Other reason?"

"Like, is there some kind of historic tension between witches and werewolves that I'm not aware of?"

Sometimes I forgot that Taliyah hadn't been raised in the supernatural community. And her job was more than just knowing how to use her powers to subdue someone or save someone else. It was also about understanding the community, and the ins and outs regarding species of supernaturals and how they interacted with other species. Taliyah still had gaps in her knowledge base, things no one thought to mention because they were things *everyone* already knew—things we took for granted. Or they were human and weren't supposed to know anything at all.

Witches weren't exactly the most popular of the supernatural species out there. We didn't take crap from anyone, we tended to exist in large covens with lots of backup, and people could get a little intimidated by our abilities, wealth, and general awesomeness. We'd never had any historical beef with werewolves, but honestly, that was probably more to do with witches not bothering to think about werewolves than anything else.

I shifted in my seat. "No. Witches and werewolves don't have particular species beefs with each other. Witches and vampires, now, that's a whole other cauldron."

That situation was still a sore spot for me. Like a bruise that I couldn't stop pressing on, even though it ached every time I did. Witches and vampires had been in a cold war since longer than even I'd been alive, and that was only because two Blood Wars had decimated both sides, and no one was really eager for a third. Witches had magic, but vampires 'reproduced' faster. Vampires were more physically powerful, but they couldn't tolerate sunlight. It was a precarious balance, and there'd been some rumblings lately that people were trying to kick the fight off yet again.

I wish I'd paid more attention to those rumors. Maybe if I had, I'd have never agreed to let Astrid go off to Blood Rose Academy, no matter how much she'd begged, bargained and pleaded. If I hadn't allowed her to attend that horrible school, if I'd insisted that the coven could teach her any and everything she needed to know, maybe she wouldn't have been attacked and turned against her will. And all by people looking to start a war.

Vampires didn't have magic. It was only through Astrid's hidden fae heritage that she'd managed to keep any of hers, but she'd never be a witch again. Even if Astrid didn't appear to have any regrets about her new vampiric condition, I did. And I knew Maverick did.

She was safe, I told myself fiercely, fisting my hands to hide their trembling. She was with her uncle, safe in a distant fae land while she learned to master her faerie magic. He would never let anything happen to her. I told myself that at night, when I woke up from nightmares in which Maverick hadn't gotten her out in time, that we'd all been too late, and she'd never risen at all. Sometimes those assurances were enough to let me get a few more hours of sleep. Sometimes.

It was a subject that was already done and there was nothing I could do about it now, so I pushed it aside and tried to focus on the here and now. Only to be reminded that Bryony was only a little older than Astrid. *Had been*, had been only a little older.

I shifted in my seat, crossing my legs the

other way. "Look, there wasn't anything magically on that nightgown that could ever hurt anyone, much less kill them. Maverick helped me with the enchantments, even. He did the embroidered spell work. And between the two of us—well, it's just not possible. If there were something that was off, one or the other of us would have noticed it."

Taliyah tapped her pen again, looking back over her notes. "Maverick told me the same thing," she admitted. "No one else has any idea how Bryony died. Her body's been collected by a," she made a face and gestured to the air. "Magical medical examiner I know. He should be able to tell if Bryony was poisoned or anything else with a toxicology screen."

"I doubt anyone would try to poison a healthy werewolf." I drummed my nails against the armrest of my uncomfortable chair. Was insufficient padding part of the interrogation technique? Let people's legs go numb until they confessed? "They're notoriously hearty. Plus, they can eat raw meat as part of their diet and with their crazy fast metabolisms, I doubt poison would do much more than give them indigestion."

"Hmm."

I frowned, thinking. "Unless she was poisoned with silver."

"Silver?" Taliyah repeated, writing it down.

I nodded. "But you would have known just by looking at her if that was the case. Silver poisoning can be... dramatic, in werewolves."

Leaning back in her chair, Taliyah's jaw worked silently, like she was arguing with herself. Finally, she reached down and opened one of her desk drawers and pulled out a file folder. She fished around inside it, and then pulled out a few sheets of paper and slid them across the desk towards me.

They were photographs, I realized. Printed on glossy paper, they were surprisingly crisp and detailed. It was the subject matter that had me sucking in a shocked breath.

They were obviously taken from the scene of the crime, and my eyes kept shying away to the edges, taking in all the little details so I wouldn't have to focus on Bryony. It was a generic motel room, other than the fact that it was actually pretty clean. The walls were a pale beige, the carpet short pile, the artwork extremely neutral. It looked like any number of out of the way little motels to be found in the area, other than the little booklet on the nightstand that welcomed travelers to the Blue Moon.

Eventually, I couldn't put it off any longer, and I dragged my attention to the body lying center stage. It was pretty much like Mrs. Reid had described, but somehow more horrible. Bryony was lying on the bed, her head on the pillows, with her hands folded primly over her stomach, like she'd laid down to take a little nap before the ceremony. Except no sleeping person looked... flat, like that. Her skin was almost waxy, all the flush drained out of her cheeks. She was in her nightgown, the one I'd worked so hard on, trying to make it perfect for her big day.

It was the stupidest thing to notice, but the nightgown hung a little funny at the bodice. I knew it was just my pride talking, but I'd taken her measurements myself. Twice. The nightgown had been made perfectly to fit her exact body, no puckers, no twisted seams. So why was it sitting like that?

I knew I was focusing on silly little details to avoid really paying attention to the fact that Bryony was dead and there she was—laid out for all the world to see (or for just Taliyah and me to see, as the case might be), but it still nagged at me.

I shoved the pictures away from me, and they fluttered across the desk back towards Taliyah.

"So, not silver poisoning," I said with a brightness I didn't feel in the slightest.

"Then, you don't have any idea what could have killed her?"

I folded my arms across my stomach, thoroughly done with the conversation. "No, I don't. I didn't see a mark on her, and I can't think of a single spell that could kill someone like that—something that wouldn't leave a trace. By all rights, she shouldn't be dead, not a healthy young werewolf."

I wanted to get up, to move, pace around, but I didn't like letting someone see my anxiety, so I let my foot bounce up and down to try and burn it off.

"Tell me about the times you interacted with her. What was said?"

"I only met her three times, and once was literally a chance meeting where I told her that her order was ready to be picked up."

"And where was that?"

"In Portland."

She scribbled that down. "What was her general manner then?"

"Um... she seemed quiet. Unassuming. You know, like most werewolves." I paused as I shook my head. "I don't understand why someone would want her dead."

Taliyah carefully gathered the photographs and tucked them back into their folder. "You say magic didn't kill her, but you're very certain she was murdered, and didn't just have a medical event."

I snorted. "Come on. I might not be a detective, but someone had to have been with her when she died. She was arranged on the bed. There's no way she fell back and folded her own arms like that."

Taliyah conceded the point, tipping her head to the side.

"Well, thank you for coming in," she said, like it had actually been a choice. "If I have any other questions, I know where to find you."

"That's it?"

"Yep."

"Do you have any other leads? Any suspects? What about that medical examiner you mentioned, what do they think about all this?"

Taliyah blinked slowly, her face back to that perfect neutral mask. "You're aware that I can't discuss ongoing investigations, Wanda."

"You don't have *any* leads?" I asked, outraged.

"Go home, Wanda. And stay away from werewolves, please." She pinched the bridge of her nose, like her head hurt. "We don't need any misunderstandings."

Clearly, she wasn't going to give me any more answers, so I stormed out of the nearly deserted police station and back to my car. At least there wasn't anyone waiting for me outside.

Taliyah might want me to sit around doing nothing, but that just wasn't going to work for me. If word started getting around that the Reid pack was accusing me of killing their daughter with an enchantment gone wrong, my business was finished. Lorcan might have money to burn, but I wasn't about to be some moochy, little house witch.

When I'd been kicked out of my coven, and I'd come to Haven Hollow, my shop was my salvation. I'd been able to use a lifetime of skill and I'd actually made a living—not just for myself, but also for Astrid. And then I'd been able to build a new coven. I couldn't just let that all circle the drain. Whoever had killed Bryony needed to be caught, and they needed to face justice so that it was clear that I had absolutely nothing to do with it.

And if Taliyah didn't have any leads, well, I'd just have to look into the mess myself.

No one was going to pin the blame on Wanda Depraysie and get away with it.

And Bryony deserved justice. She was just a girl, barely an adult, and what had happened to her wasn't right and it wasn't fair.

The steering wheel creaked under my grip, and I had to force my fingers to relax. After my second blooding, I'd become a lot stronger than I'd used to be. I was still getting accustomed to it.

My indignation managed to fuel me all the way back to Lorcan's house. I just couldn't deal with the coven house at the moment, where everyone would have questions, and I didn't have answers or the inclination to gab about it.

Lorcan's Porsche was actually in the driveway when I pulled in, which made sense, since by this point, it was only an hour until sunrise. I'd just put the car into park and killed the engine, when my door was opening of its own accord and then Lorcan leaned in, his beautiful green eyes full of concern.

"Are you alright, Sweetling?"

Well, so much for the hope that the rumors hadn't completely flooded the town yet. Werewolves had big mouths, apparently.

All at once, I was bone tired. I'd burned all of my anger to get myself home, but it suddenly felt like I had thousand-pound weights attached to each limb, and the idea of moving them was terrible.

I kept seeing Bryony lying across her bed like a posed doll, flashing through my mind. My throat felt tight. I had no idea what my face was doing, but Lorcan looked like he'd been sucker punched.

"Oh, Sweetling." His knuckles brushed against the side of my cheek, tracing the curve. "Come on. Come inside."

Lorcan reached in and unbuckled my seat belt, and then scooped me into his arms, bumping the car door shut with his hip.

He carried me so easily, cradled against his chest like something precious.

Normally, I would have commented. Maybe even demanded to be put down. But I was so tired, and I couldn't stop thinking, rolling everything over and over in my head. So, I rested my cheek against Lorcan's chest and just let him carry me into the house.

Chapter Seven

The first step in my 'prove Wanda's innocent' plan, was to make sure that the whole situation was, in fact, not my fault.

I hated the idea of it, but the truth of the matter was that my magic was unstable compared to how it had used to be. And Maverick's, goddess, his was a time bomb waiting to go off. Normally, when my spells went wonky, no one died. In fact, it was usually the opposite problem. I'd brought a zombie and a ghost back to life, and combined with my cousin, managed to give life to a *mannequin*. Bringing life to the dead was one thing. Bringing life to something that had never had the spark in the first place, was very much another.

That little tidbit wouldn't be leaving the

coven. Not if Maverick and I wanted to keep breathing, anyway. And Maverick was already on shaky ground, since most witches thought warlocks were inherently out of control and dangerous. Never mind a Blood Warlock.

So, while I absolutely believed that my spell work had nothing to do with Bryony's death, I wouldn't be able to rest until I had proven as much to myself.

I'd managed to browbeat Taliyah into giving the coven access to the nightgown. It might have been evidence, yes, but as I'd pointed out, who else was she going to get to examine it? The coven was the only source she had for magical experts, and if she thought I was a compromised source because of my involvement, then that would be the same for Maverick, too, since he'd helped me.

Finally, she'd agreed, and left the lot of us alone in a storage closet in the station, but the frosty hand print she'd left on the door when she slammed it told me she still wasn't very happy about it.

It was a tight squeeze with all of us, but we hunched around the table where the nightgown was laid out. The silk looked thin and delicate under the harsh fluorescent lighting. The drone of the bulbs was going to give me a headache, I just knew it.

Apparently, Hellcat, my odious little familiar, wasn't willing to wait for the lights to do the job, and leapt up onto the table with a disdainful sniff. "Only you, Wandellmelia, could manage to get a fertility spell so wrong that it killed the customer. What a stain on your family's history, to have produced such a second-rate hex witch."

"I *didn't* mess up the enchantment, you miserable little hairball," I hissed. "Now, get off the table before you get fur all over the evidence."

He hissed at me, but did take a dainty step back from the nightgown, before plunking his furry little butt down on the table and washing his paw like he couldn't be bothered with me. I resisted the urge to shove him off the table, but only because I had bigger problems to worry about.

My fingers twitched, wanting to smooth the fabric out and get rid of the wrinkles. "So? Impressions?"

"Hmmmm." Olga, our German born witch, leaned closer, until it almost looked like she was going to sniff the cloth. "Vat enchantments did you zay you used?"

Her familiar, Franz, a racoon in the most ridiculous miniature lederhosen, swarmed up the side of the table to peer over the edge.

Hellcat took a swipe at him, and he darted

back with an annoying, high-pitched laugh, as if the two of them were playing a game.

"Get away from me, furbag," Hellcat hissed at him. "Or I'll turn you into a frankfurter."

"Franz like zee vurst!" the raccoon called back and then started a strange little jig, which everyone ignored.

I shrugged, folding my arms over my stomach as I returned my attention to the nightgown in front of me. Anxiety was beating a loud thud inside me and I wanted to tap my foot in response, but in the small room, the sound would be far too loud.

I looked at Olga and answered her question. "We used the usual charms: glamours to hide perceived flaws and highlight best features. Though really, I only minimally used those charms. I mostly used the drape of the fabric itself to get the effect Bryony wanted."

Betanya, who had herself been a Blood Witch before she managed to kill the insane vampire who had stalked her for decades, tucked graying red hair back behind her ear. "So, the biggest spell on the nightgown is the fertility enchantment then?"

"Yes." I gestured down the length of the skirt. "I wanted it to be strong, but subtle enough that it wouldn't cause her health issues, or cause the poor girl to start having litters."

Werewolves might like large families, but not usually all at once.

Betanya nodded, approvingly. "And how did you anchor it?"

"The embroidery. Maverick helped with that part." I didn't fidget, but it was close. That was the part I was most worried about. Maverick and my magic could be explosive when they came together. Literally.

We'd brought a mannequin to life and turned her into a shapeshifter. Dear goddess, what if we'd turned a living wolfshifter into a mannequin? Bile burned at the back of my throat, and I swallowed it down, refusing to throw up on evidence. If only because Taliyah would never forgive me.

"I mean, it looks pretty good to me," Imani, our newest member, said as she held her hand just over the cloth. Her dark skin gleamed against the white silk. "The stitches are perfect. Who knew Mav was capable of being so delicate?" she joked.

Hellcat gave a quiet *harrumph*.

Poppy was still hugging the edges of the room, looking nervous. Not that there was much edge to the room. The whole thing was packed with boxes and supplies, with just enough clear space to surround the table. "I'm not sure what help I'm going to be," she said, apologetically.

"Enchantments aren't really my thing."

Since Poppy was more human than other, she operated in a gray zone, as a human who did magic. I'd insisted on including her in the coven when we'd formed circle Scapegrace, partially because it offered her protection. Supernatural folks were less likely to mess with her if they knew she had a bunch of vindictive witches in her corner. The other reason why I'd included her was because she'd earned it. Poppy was one of the best potion makers I'd ever seen, even compared to witches with centuries of experience.

The fact that she gave coven discounts didn't hurt either.

I hadn't brought her to the station because I thought she'd have some magical insight, but because she was almost unflaggingly, annoyingly chipper most of the time, and frankly, I could have used a dose of it. Not only that, but if Poppy was in front of me, that meant I could keep an eye on her and not worry something bad was happening to her. Was I a little overprotective of my BFF? Sure, but that's what happened when you were a witch who'd grown up without friends. Now that I had a best one, I had to keep her close and safe.

I waved off her comment. "Did you bring the *Uncrossing Oil*?"

"Yep, sure did." Then she paused and blinked. "Oh—you want to see if the night gown is cursed."

Just because I was pretty sure my spell hadn't gone haywire, that didn't mean someone *else* was using it as a vehicle for magical homicide. When my magic went wonky, it was hardly subtle, after all. And the nightgown had been out of my possession for a week and a half before the wedding. Anything could have been done to it.

Poppy fished a bright blue glass bottle out of her monstrous purse (which coincidentally I believed she'd purchased at a Ross Dress 4 Less—and that just couldn't happen on my watch).

"I have a Cole Haan handbag in the store that is worthy of your talents," I informed her.

She frowned. "What's wrong with my bag?"

I looked from the floppy insult she'd termed a 'bag' to her and repeated, "I have a Cole Haan handbag in the store *that is worthy of your talents*."

"Just accept it," Imani whispered to her.

Poppy's eyebrows lifted as she nodded. "Well, thanks, Wanda."

"Mmm," I responded as she then gently dabbed some of the oil inside the hem of the nightgown. We all hovered around then, waiting for the concoction to stain black if the dress was set with some kind of malicious spell, but there was nothing. Well, the fabric smelled a little bit like jasmine, but no other changes happened.

"Zo, ist not cursed," Olga announced cheerfully.

Franz laughed again, and the sound seemed to ricochet off the walls, so it was coming from every angle. Hellcat's ears flattened, and I wished I could do the same, which was very uncomfortable, because I didn't like agreeing with Hellcat on principle.

"I don't know, Wanda." Imani made another slow pass with her hand over the fabric, a little crease forming between her brows. "I don't feel anything nasty coming from it. The spells you guys used wouldn't hurt anyone."

"And no one else tampered with it," Poppy added.

Betanya hummed and tapped her finger to her bottom lip. "Perhaps we should turn the dress inside out, and examine the embroidery from the opposite side. Just to be thorough."

I was suddenly extremely glad that Maverick wasn't able to be here, due to helping Taliyah. I knew Betanya hadn't meant anything by it, wanting to examine his work more closely. But Maverick had a lot of years of not being respected in a coven, and a lot more years of being rejected by it, and he would have taken the comment as a slight to his abilities that we all would have paid for, and we would have paid for weeks.

I understood where he was coming from, at least a little. It was hard to shrug off those memories and experiences. That didn't make it one ounce less annoying, though.

But Betanya had a good point, so we carefully turned the nightgown inside out and examined the embroidery from the other side. Nothing leapt out at me. Frankly, the stitches were almost as neat as they were on the front side. There were no misplaced bits, or wrong stitches in the anchor for the fertility spell. Certainly nothing that could have banged the spell up bad enough for it to actually hurt someone, much less kill them.

It was something of a relief, but at the same time, it was baffling. Why was Bryony dead?

Hellcat sniffed. "Well, why don't we find another werewolf to try it on? If they drop dead, then at least we'll know it truly was your shoddy work."

I pinched the bridge of my nose, trying to hold back the headache blooming behind my eyes. "We're not experimenting with other werewolves."

Hellcat scoffed and stood. "This is so like you, you shriveled wench. No follow through."

He leapt down from the table and pranced out of the room. Vile little beast.

"Does anyone else have any ideas?" Frustration put an edge on my voice.

Olga and Poppy shook their heads, wide-eyed. Betanya frowned, staring down at the rumpled fabric.

Imani shrugged, the long coils of her hair sliding over her shoulders. "Sorry, Wanda. I'm fresh out of ideas."

It was a relief that it hadn't been Maverick's and my spellwork that had killed Bryony, but it also meant that I was back to square one. Because even though I knew I hadn't caused that poor girl's death, there wasn't any way I could really prove it. The Reids could just say that the coven was lying to protect me, and without bringing in another magical expert, which I didn't want to, because I wouldn't trust them, there wasn't anything else for it.

Which left me still standing as the most obvious suspect, but with a mild sense of relief that I hadn't killed someone without meaning to.

Willie-Ray, Betanya's familiar, a skunk in a sleeveless plaid shirt, stomped his feet and grumbled. "Summa bitch."

And yes, that did sum it up rather nicely.

Chapter Eight

Maverick called me that evening when the sun was just about down.

"Don't bother coming in. There hasn't been a customer all day. I'm closing up and heading out."

I froze, aghast. "Not a single customer?"

Cloth rustled as he moved, like he was switching ears. "No. Not unless you count the countless people who keep stopping and staring at me through the window, whispering to each other and scurrying away when they realize I can see them."

Wonderful. Terrific. The small-town gossip mill was already churning away, it seemed.

I closed my eyes. "Fine. Just lock up. Set the wards, I don't need people getting cute."

LACE LAMENTS

Maverick grunted and hung up, which was pretty personable where he was concerned. I, meanwhile, was having my own personal meltdown. I was going to go bankrupt at the rate things were going. I should have never let those werewolves through my front door.

Lorcan bustled through the kitchen, already in his scrubs and jacket, as he grabbed his keys off the table and paused only long enough to drop a kiss onto my head. "Running late. Got to go, Sweetling. See you later."

And then he was gone. It was astonishing that a man who could run faster than a car was always almost late for work.

I rubbed the spot where he'd kissed me and scowled. I'd been pretty distracted over the last couple days, understandably. But after the first night, when Lorcan had been so sweet and attentive, holding me all day as I finally drifted off to sleep, he'd then gone back to his frazzled, distracted, somehow exhausted self again, and if he ever held still long enough for it, I was going to give him a piece of my mind.

I was having a crisis here! And my husband was more concerned with flossing and fluoride?

To spell with it.

Analyzing the nightgown hadn't turned up anything, other than what I'd been saying all along; it was impossible that my work had killed Bryony. The trick was, getting a bunch of grieving werewolves to believe as much. They weren't going to take my or my coven's word on it, and werewolves didn't have any magic at all, which meant they wouldn't understand our explanation. Well, I supposed they knew one spell; how to turn into a wolf. It was hardly relevant, though.

So, if I couldn't prove my innocence with the evidence I had, then in order to save my business and my name as a witch, I was just going to have to dig up the guilty party.

Someone clearly wanted that poor girl dead. And in a family as co-dependent and up in each other's business as the Reid pack? Someone had to know something.

Part of the horde that had descended on my store had been made up of girls younger than Bryony, sisters and cousins, from what I'd pieced together. Now, granted, I didn't have a good relationship with my sisters, they'd tried to kill me a couple of times, but I had it on fairly good authority that a lot of people were close to their siblings, and even confided in them.

Lurking around the school wasn't doable. Partly because I couldn't go out during the day, and partly because I was fairly sure I'd get reported. So, that left after school. Where did children go when they weren't being put through the hell of the mortal education system?

I could ask Sybil, but she tended to travel with her own small, tight knit group. Instead, I sent a text to Poppy.

Where do children hang around after school?

I got back an extremely unhelpful '*?*' in response.

My lips flattened together in frustration. What was she not understanding? Poppy's son, Finn, was a young teenager. Surely, she knew where he went when he wasn't with her?

I mean, if I needed to find a child, where would I look for one?

The little line of dots floated across my screen for far, far too long as Poppy wrote and backspaced and wrote again. Finally, a response popped up.

???!

She had to be doing this on purpose. I tapped the keyboard, a little harder than necessary. *Can you ask Finn where kids like to hang out after school?*

And finally, something actually useful popped up. *Finn says that Sweeter Haunts is a popular spot. Do I get to know why you're hunting for children?*

Ah, Sweeter Haunts. Haven Hollow's Halloween themed candy shop. I should have known. I sent Poppy back a text that just said '*no*', and then ignored my phone buzzing as I shoved it into my purse and grabbed my keys.

It was time to get some answers.

***

The Main Street of Haven Hollow was the beating heart of town. Wanda's Witchery was there, of course, right across the street from Poppy's Potions. There was also Stomper's Creamery, where centaur Stanley Stomper sold the best ice cream I'd ever tasted. Just down the road was the Half-Moon Bar and Grill, owned by Roy, a fellow Council member and Sasquatch. It was the best burger in town, had live music on occasion, and was the go-to hangout for the magical crowd.

And then, of course, there was Sweeter Haunts, where it was October thirty-first, all year round. Chocolate cauldrons and marshmallow ghosts hung in the window, and just beyond them I could see the orange and black checkered tile of the floor. Someone had added some cotton candy spider webs, with a huge gummy spider in the center. I made a mental note to grab some chocolate before I headed out. After the week I was having, I deserved a sugar bomb if I wanted it.

True to Finn's intel, the place was swarming with teens and pre-teens. If they weren't perusing the aisles, they were sitting at the soda fountain at the back. It was almost nostalgic, though I didn't ever remember being able to get a black charcoal milkshake back in the fifties. I'd have to double check with Libby.

The clientele was a mixed bag: some human and some not so human, but I finally managed to spot a few familiar faces clustered together by one of the stools.

Bingo.

Two sisters, and a cousin of Bryony's. I racked my brain, trying to remember their names. The youngest sister was Casey, I was pretty sure, but I drew a blank for the other two. Still, they were my best shot at getting some information on Bryony's life, what with her adult relatives up in arms. Even if the kids blamed me, I figured I could probably bully them into telling me what I needed to know.

I marched up on them before they realized who I was. The cousin's eyes widened, and she vanished down an aisle. The older sister looked like she wished she could do the same, but was stuck between the wall and the stool her younger sister was perched on. The littlest one just glared at me, her jaw set. And I believe she growled.

"I need to talk to you," I told them, subtly barring the way. I wasn't about to trap literal children, but I also didn't want to make it too easy to run.

The youngest girl's nose wrinkled up, her freckles all but vanishing. The older sister ducked her head, avoiding my eyes.

"We're not supposed to talk to you," she mumbled into her chest.

"Right." I crossed my arms, my hip jutting to one side. "Listen, I'm very sorry for your loss. I can't imagine what you must be going through. But I didn't hurt Bryony. You need to know that. I didn't have any reason to."

A quick glance, but then her gaze planted itself on the ground again. Werewolves. I gritted my teeth.

The youngest one was bolder, meeting my eyes squarely. If she'd been a few years older, I wouldn't have bothered with her sister. But interrogating someone in elementary school was a bit much, even for me.

"She was your sister," I continued. "You probably knew her best in the world." I glanced between both of them. "You have to know who might have wanted to hurt her."

"You—" the younger one started.

I shook my head. "I didn't do this. And the

more your family focuses on me, the more likely it is that the person who did do it, is going to get away with it."

Casey—yeah, I was almost positive her name was Casey—scowled. Her little jaw thrust forward into the most mulish expression I'd ever seen, outside of a mirror. The older girl glanced at me again, and then swallowed hard enough that I saw her throat bob. Her eyes were reddened, like she'd been crying.

"There... there's this man. He and dad, they don't get along."

Casey growled again. "Marianne, shut up."

Marianne, that was her name.

Marianne swallowed again, but kept talking. "They're kind of rivals. I don't know, but he might have... have hurt Bryony to get at dad."

That sounded, as they said in the crime solving business, like a lead. "Does this guy have a name?"

Marianne glanced at Casey, who was glaring but silent, and nodded tentatively. "Victor. Victor Lewis."

Finally, a hint. But still, that seemed kind of a stretch. They might not get along, but would he really kill the man's daughter on her wedding day just to hurt him?

Bryony hadn't seemed super thrilled about her upcoming wedding. And from the small amount I remembered from the wedding itself, the groom hadn't looked like it was the best day of his life, either.

So, I pressed my advantage. "What about the groom?"

Marianne frowned, confused enough to actually meet my eyes for a split second. "Jackson?"

"I guess."

She nodded. "What about him?"

I shrugged and adjusted my purse strap. "The marriage didn't hit me as a love match. How were things between the bride and groom?"

Marianne shuffled and darted a glance around her, like she was looking for an escape route. If the situation hadn't been so dire, I might have felt guilty about hounding her for information. Maybe. Her family had accused me of murder, though. Or of being so bad at my job that I'd killed someone. I wasn't sure which was worse, honestly.

Casey gave her sister a fierce look. It was impressive, especially from a twelve-year-old. But it wasn't up to witch standards.

Marianne all but folded in on herself. "Jackson... he didn't really want to get married, at first. But his family convinced him."

Casey snorted, rolling her eyes. "Bullied him, you mean."

"Why?" I glanced between the girls. "Why were they so set on him marrying Bryony?"

Marianne shrugged. "They weren't. Not specifically. It was just, Jackson had a girlfriend, before the engagement. But his family didn't like her."

Well, that would have been good to know about. "Why not?"

"She's not a werewolf." Marianne stared at the floor like she was trying to memorize the orange and black pattern. "They wanted him to settle down, raise some cubs. He couldn't do that with his girlfriend, so they convinced him to get married to Bryony."

She blinked rapidly, her eyes shiny with tears as she spoke her sister's name.

I knew I should go. I'd already moved to take a step back. Yes, I wanted to know what was going on, but bullying children wasn't how I enjoyed spending my time. Especially like this. Young witches at least grew up knowing how to fight back. They'd give as good as they got, for the most part.

I hesitated, though. "Do you know Jackson's ex-girlfriend's name?"

"No." Marianne shook her head. "I've never met her. I just heard Jackson's parents complaining about her."

Casey was glaring at me, her little teeth

bared, leaning forward on her stool like she was going to launch herself at me if I didn't back off. It was pretty heartening, actually. I hoped she kept that fighting spirit. Werewolves could use a shaking up.

But right then, it was time for a retreat.

"Thank you. Again, I'm sorry about Bryony."

Marianne nodded, her arms wrapped around herself as she stared at the ground. She'd tilted her head so that the long fall of her brown hair hid her face from me, but I was pretty sure she was crying silently.

I turned to leave, and I could feel Casey Reid's eyes boring into my back my entire way out of the store.

Uneasiness rolled around in my belly. It felt a bit like guilt. Lucky for me, I had years of practice ignoring that kind of thing, because I had a murder to solve. And I decided I'd solve it not only for myself, but for those two girls, as well.

Chapter Nine

Victor Lewis, Werewolf, wasn't a hard man to track down.

He owned and operated a car wash over on Gerrard, in the east end of town. The only trouble was, the place wasn't open after dark, so I had to be ready to spring out the door the second the sun was low enough to be considered nighttime, but still give me time to get over there before closing time. Hopefully, Victor had a ton of paperwork or something to keep him late.

It wasn't hard to slip out the door, since Lorcan hadn't come home that morning.

Oh, he'd called me, so very apologetic and had said something about an emergency that had come up, and it was too late to make the drive safely, so he was going to spend the day in the hearse with Marty driving him around town. It just couldn't be helped.

I'd hung up the phone with more force than should probably have been used against a touch screen. I didn't know what was up with the undead idiot, but I had enough problems on my plate without him shoveling on more like a side dish. I'd deal with whatever the spell was going on with him when I wasn't being accused of murder.

At least the annoyance kept me from focusing too much on the sick feeling settling into my stomach. I really didn't like feeling uneasy or insecure. Something was up with Lorcan. That was very, very obvious. And I was fairly sure he thought I was buying his lame excuses —something which made me all the angrier. I mean—how dumb did he think I was?! The absolute penis-head.

I had too much to do, so I bundled up my bad mood, and decided to make it Victor Lewis's problem.

The lot was dark when I arrived, but luckily for me, the lights were still on in the little office off to the side of the wash bays. I pulled my car up right near the door and parked.

Night wasn't really any kind of barrier for witches. But ever since my blooding, especially the second one, while I didn't go up like a Roman candle at the first hint of sunlight, I was a lot more comfortable at night. The shadows just kind of seemed to drape around me like the most luscious silk, soft and smooth. Even if someone had still been there, I doubted they would have seen me as I made my way to the office door.

It was unlocked, because of course it was. What did big, burly werewolf men have to fear from someone coming into the office? Victor was the top dog, the predator. Nothing could touch him in his territory.

Even without seeing it, I knew the smile that twisted my lips wasn't a very nice one.

The man hunched over the desk was middle aged, graying, and completely oblivious to everything going on around him that wasn't the spreadsheet on the computer before him. He poked at the keyboard with two fingers, which explained why he was still there after closing time. At the rate he was going, it must have taken him hours to balance the books.

It was a little embarrassing that he hadn't noticed me. The room wasn't big. With the desk, the werewolf, and the stacked-up boxes of cleaning solutions, rags, and what looked like more paperwork, I practically had to stand on his shoulders.

In my head, I'd planned it all out. I'd wait until he noticed me lurking, and then I could interrogate him and see if he'd really done something to Bryony just to get back at his rival. But as it turned out, standing there behind an oblivious werewolf got really boring, really fast. I did have other things to accomplish. Would it kill the man to turn his head?

Not in the mood for waiting games, I whispered a few words that had the shadows pooling thicker, darker, crowding in the corners of the room. Victor still didn't notice, even when he had to hunch forward so far that his nose was practically pressed against the monitor screen.

A bit of power and a gesture had an icy wind blowing in through the cracked open window. It caused the loose papers of his desk to flutter around the room, and Victor's breath began steaming in the air. That, finally, got his attention, but in the dumbest way possible.

He sat back with a scowl, watching his breath exhale in fog and float towards the ceiling. "Did someone turn on the air-conditioning?" he yelled out as he shook his head and continued grumbling to himself, "do those idiots think I'm made of money?"

He spun around to stand up, caught sight of me lounging behind him, and immediately fell back into his chair.

"Who the hell are you?" he sputtered, surprise quickly turning into anger.

"That's not important right now, Victor. Can I call you Victor?" I gave him a sweet smile he didn't return. "Anyway, Victor, I'm here to ask you about something."

"What the—"

"Uh uh uh," I said and waved my index finger in front if his face. "Don't you know it's rude to interrupt someone when they haven't finished speaking?" He grumbled something unintelligible. "Anyway, I'm sure you know what I want to discuss with you. I'd just like to first know why you did it. And, secondly, the obligatory question: did you really think you'd get away with it?" I buffed my nails against my shirt and made a tsking sound. "Not smart."

I might have gone soft with Marianne and Casey, on account of them being literal children. But Victor was an adult, and kind of a dumb one if his situational awareness was anything to go by. I figured I'd push hard and see what fell out.

He scowled, his teeth barred. "I have no idea what you're talking about. Now, get out of my office, whoever the hell you are."

I shook my head sadly. "Oh, Victor, don't try to lie to me. You're not very good at it. So, let's try this again, and this time: how about you stop wasting both our time?"

A dull red color snaked up his neck and into his face as Victor Lewis shot to his feet and tried to use his height to intimidate me. "I don't know who the hell you think you are, but you're going to get out of my office, or I'll toss you out."

Posture, posture, threat display. Werewolf 101. Yawn.

Now, I hadn't planned on using any stronger magic against Mr. Lewis. Partly because I wasn't sure he'd actually done anything to deserve it, but also because my magic was still a bit, well, *volatile*, to put it politely. I didn't want to hurt him, much, or turn him into a teacup poodle or something, though that would have been hilarious, all the same.

But that didn't mean I wasn't willing to use the smaller bits of power. Three hissing words, and the shadows surged up to yank him back into his chair.

Ha, in your face, Hellcat, I thought to myself. *I'm not all raising the dead and blood bolts.*

The flush in Victor's face drained away, along with every other speck of color that had been there. He stared up at me, sweat beading on his brow. "You're a witch?"

"Really? Took you that long?"

"What do you want?"

I examined my nails. The mulberry polish I'd painted them with was starting to chip. I'd have to get a manicure soon. "I already told you, Victor. Are you really going to make me repeat myself?"

"No, but–" He swallowed, looking like he might actually be sick. "Why do you care? It was just business!"

I froze, suddenly so angry that I couldn't breathe around the surge of rage in my chest. I had to take a careful breath, because for a second, I thought I might actually spit fire if I opened my mouth.

A girl was dead. Far too young, and on what was supposed to be her happiest day, a celebratory day. She'd been robbed of everything—her future, her happiness, her life. And it was just business?

My smile had way too many teeth in it, and Victor was wolf enough to know it for the threat it was.

"Just business? Alright, Victor, I'm curious. Exactly how much business was that girl's life worth?"

He froze, his brow furrowing like he was trying really hard to think. "Wait, what? "

I leaned forward, getting too close to his face. "Did you work it out on a calculator? Exactly what it was worth to kill Bryony?"

Victor reared back, alarmed as he held up his hands and shook his head. "Wait, wait, wait, I didn't kill anyone! What are you talking about?"

"I'm talking about the murder of Bryony Reid, apparently your enemy's daughter," I snapped. "Keep up."

"I didn't kill Bryony!" Victor stared at me, aghast. "I thought you were talking about the land plot, over by the Blue Moon."

What in spell was he now going on about? My patience, never one of my many virtues, strained a little thinner. "Explain. Quickly would be best."

Victor pulled a rag off the corner of the desk and mopped some of the sweat off his face. It left a big smear of what I assumed was car polish on his forehead, but I wasn't about to tell him that.

"Okay. There's this big plot of land, just west of the motel that went up for sale, right?" Victor made a vague gesture towards the wall, like he was directing me. "Tom wanted it, so he could build a swimming pool or some crap, I don't know. But that's good land, so I maybe slipped someone a few bucks to make sure the owner sold to me instead."

I must have been making some kind of unpleasant expression, because Victor blanched.

"L-look, I wanted to build another car wash, with a fuel station. That area gets a lot of traffic, especially for tourists, right? It's just business. Sure, Reid didn't like it, but them's the breaks, right? I didn't touch his kids. I wouldn't do that. Especially not a female. She was cub-bearing age, yeah? I wouldn't have hurt her! You gotta believe me."

And just like that, I went from mildly irritated at wasting my time, to maybe wanting to see if I could actually scare him into wetting his pants. Cub-bearing age? Ugh. Because that would be the only reason it wasn't okay to murder a young woman.

Whatever. Clearly, Victor didn't have anything relevant to share with me, and I'd already been stuck in that room with him long enough. The overwhelming smell of sweat, stale coffee, and whatever cheap cologne Victor was wearing was giving me a headache. I wanted out of there. And to maybe take a shower. Or three. I didn't even bother with forcing him to sit through a witch's version of a polygraph test. I could see the truth right there on his face. He wasn't guilty.

"Ugh," I groaned and gave him a frown that said I was annoyed I'd wasted my time.

Relief set in on his face, and a hint of the arrogance he'd had when I first showed up. Victor's lip curled up, ever so slightly, and I knew he was going to try and mouth off, to get back some of his own, so that when he regaled his canine buddies about what had happened, he could spin it like he'd scared some 'little witch' off.

Before he could open his mouth and try my patience any further, I leaned forward, bringing our faces close.

"If I find out you were lying to me, Victor? Instead of a wolf, you'll be turning into a Pekinese on the next full moon."

He wilted back into his chair, proverbial tail tucked between his knees.

Had I needed to do that? No. But it did make me feel a little better when I stalked out of the office to get back in my car.

One suspect down, and the night was still young.

***

I eventually tracked down Jackson, the groom, slumped over a bar stool at the Half-Moon Bar and Grill.

It was a quiet night, as far as things were ever quiet here, long after the dinner rush, with no live performances booked. Jackson was propped up with one hand under his chin and surrounded by so many empty bottles that anyone who wasn't a werewolf would have been on route to the hospital.

Roy was tending the bar and keeping an eye on Jackson, if the way he was polishing the same glass over and over was any indication. He nodded when he saw me and jerked a head towards the semi-aware werewolf when he saw where I was heading.

"He yours?"

I made a face, wrinkling up my nose. "Spell no. I just need to talk to him."

Roy shrugged, tossing the pristine dish cloth over one shoulder as he went to busy himself at the other end of the bar. "Tell him he's cut off."

I lifted a hand in answer and slid onto the barstool one over from Jackson. The smell of alcohol slapped me in the face as I sat, and I almost gagged at how strong it was. First Victor's cologne, and now this. How did creatures with enhanced senses go around dousing themselves with such horrid smells? Or was it like with dogs, where they could roll in rotting fish and act like it was Coco Chanel? Thank the Goddess I hadn't been born a were.

I grabbed a couple of coasters off the bar and made a rudimentary fan in order to (not so subtly) try and bat the smell back in the direction it was coming from.

"Jackson?" I finally prodded when it became extremely obvious that he was off in his own little world and probably hadn't even noticed me sitting down.

It took him a second, but then he twisted around to face me and almost fell off the stool in the process. He blinked, one of his eyes closing slower than the other. "Who're you?"

I sighed, feeling really put upon. Dealing with drunks while sober was never fun. It might go a little better if I got a few cocktails of my own, but then that would mean that I was drinking with a potential murderer, and that just didn't seem like a good idea. Plus, I had to drive home. And I'd already had one car accident that had nearly killed me, so I wasn't in the market for another one.

So, none for me. But why was Jackson tying it on so hard for a girl he hadn't even wanted to marry? Was this what a guilty conscience looked like? Or was this just a normal Wednesday evening for him?

One thing that did appear fairly obvious: he wasn't really in any state to be questioned. Then again, I wasn't a cop. And besides, wasn't there something to the old saying *in Vino Veritas*? There was truth in wine. Maybe he'd spill something good, and I could dump it all on

Taliyah and go home and sleep for about a week.

"Who I am isn't important." He probably wouldn't remember it even if I introduced myself, so why bother? "I want to talk about you."

"Me?" I could almost see the thoughts limping their sotted way across his brain. The poor things were struggling hard. "Talk about what?"

He hiccupped, lurching on his stool. I'd always assumed that was just something that happened in cartoons.

Drunk people could be unpredictable, so I'd have to watch my step, at least a little. Jackson might be an angry drunk and start something that would get us both booted out of the bar. Or he might be a weepy drunk, like Roy's girlfriend, Fifi. She was oddly morose after a few cocktails, especially for a succubus. Usually when the Black Cat Cocktail Club met up, by the end of the night, at least one of us would end up patting her consolingly on the back for some reason or other. On one memorable occasion, it had been because the frog drawn on the label of a bottle of rum had looked 'sad', whatever the spell that meant.

As far as I was concerned, tears were worse than anger, or at least more annoying. If Jackson got fighty, Roy was less than ten feet away, and as a Sasquatch, he was quite capable of hurling a werewolf Jackson's size out the door like a javelin. Actually, that might be entertaining to watch...

"Well, Jackson. I'd like to talk to you about a wedding."

A provocative statement? Maybe. But I wanted answers, and I didn't have all night to get them. He'd either get mad, confused, or weepy, and then at least I'd know what to do to handle it.

Jackson stared down at his hands for a long time, then picked up one of the bottles in front of him and tried to take a sip, only to thump it back down on the bar when he realized it was empty.

"Wedding's canceled," he mumbled, running a hand over his face. "No bride."

He was hard to read, as soused as he was. He wasn't gloating, but he also wasn't acting like it was tragic, so it was hard to get a pin on where to go from there.

"And how do you feel about that?"

Jackson tried to catch Roy's eye, lifting his bottle up like a child trying to get a parent to notice a boo-boo. Roy angled himself away, pretending not to notice, and Jackson slumped down on his stool, crestfallen.

"My parents were right." He wobbled, a little precariously, and I thought for a second, he was going to collapse onto the floor, but he righted himself at the last moment. "It's time for me to get serious. To settle down with a woman who can give me cubs."

Cringe. I made a face, but Jackson didn't seem to notice.

"I thought that woman was going to be Bryony. It sucks that she's dead. I mean, as women go, she seemed okay."

Well, I hoped Jackson wasn't in charge of the girl's eulogy. Jesus.

Jackson swayed again. "I even broke up with my girlfriend to be with Bryony. Wouldn't be right, getting married when I was still dating someone else, you know?"

I stared at the half-wit and thought for a second about cursing him to grow a tail. But that probably wouldn't go well, especially since Roy basically was the Council, and they got unreasonably naggy about blatant usage of magic in public. Spoilsports.

I drummed my nails against the bar, wanting the whole conversation over. "Was your girlfriend upset?"

"Brooke?" Jackson blinked again, leaning ever so slightly sideways. "Oh, she was devastated. It broke her heart. Poor girl."

Who could blame someone for being upset about losing out on this charmer? "Was Brooke human?"

Jackson wrinkled his nose up. "What? No. She's a nymph."

That was interesting. I was surprised that Jackson could pull a nymph, but then again, I wasn't seeing him at his best, maybe. Hopefully. "Did you hurt Bryony, Jackson?"

"What?"

"So you and Brooke could still be together?"

His eyes widened, and he lurched in a way that made me scramble clear in case he was going to puke.

Jackson grabbed for my wrist, hanging off my arm with both hands. "No! God no! I'd never hurt Bryony. She was–" He belched and tried again. "She was going to be the mother of my cubs."

Now *I* was going to puke. Way to reduce an entire person's life solely to their ability to pump out puppies. Blech.

But he seemed sincere. And I had a new possible lead in Brooke the Nymph. A jealous ex would have motivation to do away with a rival, and growing up in a coven made me extremely aware of just what lengths a petty woman would go to.

Still, it was a shame. Two interrogations and not one confession. I'd really thought this would all have wrapped up a little quicker than it was.

As to the drunk? I was pretty sure he wasn't lying. To be honest, I wasn't sure he had enough brain cells left to come up with a lie.

"Aright, well, this has been disappointing." I straightened out my skirt and tossed my hair back. "Maybe call someone to come and pick you up before Roy pours you into a bucket."

I turned and stalked out of the bar, with just a wave of goodbye to Roy. I would have been a bit more personable to Jackson, he'd just lost his bride after all, but considering the best he could drag up was that she 'seemed fine', I doubted it was a love for the ages. And, besides, he was a moron.

I did a little bit of stewing on my way back to Lorcan's. As much as I wanted to keep going, keep hunting down whoever was responsible, the sun wouldn't be long in rising. Plus, Nymphs tended to be day-time people, and I doubted one would be particularly chatty if I banged on her door at quarter to sunrise.

And, okay, yes, I was a little annoyed that I'd checked my phone before I pulled away from Roy's, and Lorcan hadn't texted me—not even once. I wasn't home, and he didn't even know it. The undead jerk.

I wanted to solve this case, fix my reputation, and maybe get Bryony some actual justice, since she seemed to be surrounded by people who only cared about her in so far as what she could give them.

And then I could go kick my husband in the butt until he told me what the spell was going on with him.

What I definitely did not need was to turn down one of the side streets, only to find a tree down across the road.

"Son of a witch," I hissed between my teeth. Where had it come from? There hadn't been any storms, and no wind above a gentle breeze. But there it was, looking like the victim of a tornado, blocking both lanes, and too big for my car to drive over without ripping into the undercarriage like a chainsaw.

Ugh, I did not need this. I threw the Escalade into reverse, figuring I'd just take another street and loop around. It would be slow and annoying, but I'd still get home in time to miss the sunrise.

Before I could start backing up to turn around, I saw a flash of movement in the trees on either side of the road. Close to a dozen men then stepped out into the road, surrounding my car and effectively boxing me in.

I was trapped.

Chapter Ten

What the spell was going on? Who were these people?

I caught a glimpse of one of them in the car headlights, and his eyes backwashed gold. Werewolves, then.

The few faces I could make out were familiar. I was pretty sure I'd seen them all at the wedding. And, yes, there was the man who'd been comforting Thea after Bryony had been discovered—Mr. Reid himself. Wonderful.

Three guesses why a bunch of Bryony's male relatives would come to talk to me on a deserted road at night, and the first two didn't count. Well, if it was a fight they wanted, then frankly, I was game. I'd been simmering in my frustrations all night, and I wasn't about to take the fall for something I hadn't done. Plus, it seemed like I was the only one who cared enough to figure out who had really killed Bryony.

They weren't here for justice. They were here because their egos had been hurt. True, I was here to clear my name, mostly, but Bryony was their family member, for spells sakes.

Well, I wasn't quite sure how that bunch of meatheads thought their little ambush was going to go, but I also wasn't interested in playing. The mild catharsis I might get from cursing them to next Tuesday wasn't worth the aggravation.

Instead, I threw the Escalade into reverse, and then floored it.

My car lurched backwards, and for a second, I thought the idiots were actually going to stand their ground and get run over. It seemed that they'd gone ahead and pooled their collective braincells, though, and bailed out of the way at the last second.

One of the younger, more impulsive ones lunged after my car as I sailed by, his hands twisted into a wolf's claws. I almost gave the little idiot a jaunty little toot of farewell with my horn, but then I heard it.

The crunch of metal. And then, when I kept moving, the side of my car gave a tortured scream, steel and fiberglass ripping apart. Son of a witch!

All the blood drained out of my face, only for it to slam back into my cheeks as rage ignited behind my rib cage.

My Escalade! Those *idiots*. They'd ripped my car!

I slammed on the brakes and threw it into park before I burst out the door. "What the spell is wrong with you? Do you have any idea how much a car like this *costs*?"

To be fair, even I didn't know. Lorcan had gifted it to me. That didn't give anyone the right to trash it, though.

I caught sight of the side panel and just about screamed. He'd dug his claws in and ripped through the back door, almost all the way to the gas tank. It was ruined. I didn't even know if that kind of thing could be fixed. Oh, I was taking that mess out on someone's hide. You bet your ass.

Mr. Reid stepped up, and growled. His teeth looked way too long and sharp for his human mouth. "You killed my daughter. You think I give a damn about your car?"

Yeah, that was pretty much where I'd thought the talk was going to go. I didn't have a lot of hope that attempting to reason with them was going to get me very far—not with the cloud of fury they were all walking around in, but I gave it a shot, anyway.

"I did not hurt Bryony. None of the spells on her nightgown were even slightly dangerous. Whoever killed her, it wasn't me."

A low, basso growl I could feel in my chest, even from several feet away, was my only answer.

I could have tried again. I could have gone for reason, done my best to deescalate the situation. But I'd been under a lot of stress, lately, partially because of the Reids and their rumor mongering. I had sympathy, grief does things to people, but they'd also just ripped the heck out of my car. So, maybe I didn't try as hard as I could have to avoid the fight they were all itching for.

The first one to charge with a snarl was a younger male, maybe Bryony's cousin or brother. He was fast, strong, as most wolves were, even in their human shapes. I let him get about a half a dozen steps from me before I launched a blood bolt into his chest and knocked him flying back into the trees.

I didn't want to seriously hurt anybody, but that didn't mean I was going to let them hurt me, either. My magic roiled beneath the surface, feeling like a lightning storm pressing against the inside of my skin. It was times like this when I noticed such a big difference from before I was blooded. As a witch, my magic would seep out and connect with the living things around me.

As a Blood Witch, my emotions, especially my anger, tended to whip things up into a frenzy. Like my magic was eager to lash out, to have a target to sink its teeth into. Sometimes it was harder to hold back, the power turning scalding, like it would burn me from the inside if I didn't erupt like a volcano first.

Watching their relative go flying apparently didn't convince the others to back off, because two more rushed me, their hands twisted into claws, their eyes backwashing gold in the headlights. No one had slipped their shape, yet, but I didn't know how long that would hold out.

Two more blood bolts, two more airborne werewolves. I winced as one of them hit a tree, which broke with a crack like a gunshot, and then just kept sailing.

Then it was Mr. Reid's turn. He came at me, his face twisted by grief and fury, teeth barred. I didn't want to hurt the man. I didn't even much want to fight him, in spite of his dumbass relative turning my car into a convertible. I mean, the man had just lost his daughter.

But the magic sang beneath my skin, coiling down my arms like bloody ribbons to twine around my fingers. I didn't want to lash out, not at a grieving father, but from the look on his face, he wasn't going to give me any choice. He came at me in a rush, almost too fast to see, and I braced my knees, power pooling into my hands, waiting to be thrown.

Before I could do more than twitch, there was a blur of shadows, and Mr. Reid went sailing off into the woods, skidding across the wet leaves.

Everyone froze. There was a gust of air, and another werewolf went flying. I shoved my hair back out of my face, trying to understand what was happening, but things were happening faster than I could follow.

When a good half of the gathered wolves had been sent flying into the night, they finally seemed to realize something was going on and started to back away. There was another rush of wind, and between one blink and the next, Lorcan was by my side.

Lorcan prided himself on his ability to blend in with humanity. Thanks, at least partly, to his Irish charm, he was actually better at it than I was. He lived his life as normally as possible, running his dental clinic and taking care of all the pearly whites in Haven Hollow.

Even after everything we'd been through, he didn't normally get much more than annoyed.

Standing there beside me now though, in the dark, facing down a pack of werewolves, he was furious.

I'd never seen him look so much like a vampire. His eyes almost glowed in the dark as he snarled, fangs on display. He hunched forward, like a lion ready to pounce, a vicious reminder that he was just as much a predator as they were.

He tipped his chin down and snarled through his fangs. "Leave."

It was unfairly hot.

It was also apparently enough for the Reid pack to realize that they weren't going to be winning this particular fight. After they hauled their fallen members up off the ground, they retreated to the woods, growling threats all the while.

"This isn't over." Mr. Reid glared at me as his relatives dragged him off.

I waited until they were gone before I turned to Lorcan, wondering if I could coax him home to bed for some quality time before dawn. I'd just opened my mouth when he rounded on me, still furious.

"What the bloody hell were you thinking?"

My mouth closed so fast that my teeth clicked together. Not quite sated, the fury in my blood reared back up like a snake about to strike. "Excuse me?"

"Fighting with werewolves, out where God and anyone could have seen you." He raked a hand back through his hair, making it stand up in places. "You're supposed to be a vampire now, if you'd bother to remember, Wanda. And here you are, out flinging your magic around like you forgot what in the hell *you're supposed to be!*"

When Lorcan got worked up, his brogue tended to get thicker. Normally, it was attractive as hell, but in that moment, it just made me want to punch him even harder than I already wanted to punch him.

"I was *thinking* I didn't want to get mauled by werewolves out for revenge." I folded my arms across my chest, and ignored the cold, squirming feeling settling into my stomach. "What exactly did you want me to do? Offer to arm wrestle them? Am I not supposed to defend myself?"

He growled, frustrated. "Of course, you are. But do you have to be so bloody obvious about it?"

I flung my arms out to the sides, gesturing to the woods, the road, the tree in front of my car. "We're in the middle of nowhere! And I didn't pick it, thank you. I didn't go looking for a fight. I'm just trying to figure out who murdered Bryony Reid. All by myself, I might add, since someone's been too busy with his own head up his ass to notice anything else around him!"

That took some of the wind out of Lorcan's sails, and he visibly sagged. "I told you, things at the clinic–"

"You're not in your scrubs, Lorcan." I glared at him, feeling the hot press of tears at the corner of my eyes and hating it. "You weren't at the office, so don't pretend like you were. Spare me that insult, at least."

It had taken me a minute, in all the chaos, to notice that instead of his usual scrubs and jacket that he wore home from work, Lorcan was in slacks and a mulberry shirt that I'd picked out for him, since it made his eyes look like emeralds. He'd thrown a long wool coat over it all, but it was a far cry from surgical gear.

Lorcan froze for a second, like a jammed sewing machine, before stuttering back to life. "I changed when I got home, and I heard fighting."

I looked away. I was cold and tired, and I just wanted to go home. Not get attacked and then yelled at for protecting myself. "Sure."

Lorcan gave a gusty exhale, his shoulders sagging. "I'm sorry, Sweetling. Are you alright? I didn't mean to bark at you. You just scared me."

I wasn't injured, so I nodded. 'Fine' might not have been the word I'd have used to describe how I was feeling, what with my magic still roiling beneath my skin, itching to be set free, but it was close enough. I was too tired to deal with anything else for the night. Too tired to even demand where the spell he'd been. But at the moment, I didn't care.

"Let's get you home, then." Lorcan reached out and laid a tentative hand on my shoulder. When I didn't bite him or shrug it off, he tugged me closer to his body.

I stayed stiff in his arms, but allowed it. "I don't think my car is going to make it home."

The werewolf had really done a number on it. The jerk.

"We can send a tow truck for it tomorrow." He tugged me forward. "Let's go, Sweetling. The sun will be up soon."

Lorcan was a lot faster than I was, so I let him scoop me up in his arms and hurry me through the woods. The day felt like it was dragging off my shoulders, long and heavy. I hadn't really learned anything worthwhile, and I still didn't have any idea who would have wanted to kill Bryony, or why.

And I was still pissed with Lorcan, and whatever it was he was hiding from me. But just for the moment, I let myself be tired, and I promised myself I could figure everything out tomorrow.

Chapter Eleven

Someone was pounding on my door.

I jerked my head up from the pillow, and tried to shove all my hair out of the way so I could see, and breathe, again. A baleful glare at the clock told me that it was still almost a half an hour to sunset, which explained why Lorcan was still passed out beside me, not even twitching at the fact that someone was doing a battering ram impression with the front door.

The previous day came back to me in a rush, and my head dropped forward into my hands as I groaned. I still wasn't any closer to finding the killer, and now I had angry werewolves out for revenge, and Lorcan was being even weirder than he normally was.

Whoever it was knocked so hard that the

house shook.

"Alright, alright, give me a minute," I shouted, grabbing my robe.

"Someone had better be dying," I muttered as I stalked through the hall. My steps stuttered, and I tripped, righting myself against the wall. When I finally got to the door and wrenched it open, it occurred to me that maybe I should have checked who it was first, what with the vengeful werewolves and all. Luckily for me, it was just Taliyah.

Maybe not so luckily, if she was here to arrest me.

"Taliyah," I greeted her, warily. "Why are you trying to kick my door in? This is becoming kind of a bad habit."

Instead of saying 'hello', or, 'sorry for the big bad wolf wake up call', Taliyah just stepped up and pushed her way past me. "I need to talk to you."

I snorted, closing the door behind her as she stalked down the hall towards the living room. "Please, come on in. No, no, I insist."

Taliyah wasn't really one for jokes, even when she was off the clock. But it was very much Police Chief Morgan who sat down at the seldom used table in the kitchen, and set a very official looking manila envelope down in front of her.

I eyed the envelope like most people would a bucket of scorpions, but I took the seat opposite her. "Taliyah, it's not even sundown. What is this about?"

Taliyah's face twisted up with frustration, and some other emotion I couldn't place. "I have the results of Bryony Reid's autopsy here. I need you to look at some pictures."

I'd been thinking about putting some coffee on, to see if that would help clear out some of the cobwebs in my brain, but Taliyah's words made my stomach lurch in a way that meant it was probably for the best I didn't have anything in there.

I stared at her. "You want me... To look at autopsy photos."

She nodded, one short, sharp slice of her chin.

What the spell? I wasn't exactly squeamish. Most witches weren't, the covens saw to that. But that didn't mean I wanted to look at graphic pictures of a dead body. I was gearing up to say, not just no, but spell no, when Taliyah pushed the envelope towards me and said one word.

"Please."

It really must have been the magic word, because I found myself opening the envelope and sliding the glossy photos into my hand with the kind of disgusted caution of someone handling toxic waste.

I forced myself to look at the images and then glared at Taliyah. "Is this a joke?"

"I wish it was," she answered ardently. "But no."

The photos were clearly taken in a morgue. If I squinted, I could see all the trappings—from the gurneys to the medical equipment. But the focus of the pictures was the gurney in the foreground, where a white sheet had been rolled back to reveal a pile of green and yellow leaves. There were a few thinner branches, and even a couple acorns rolling around on the metal table.

No body.

I looked back up at Taliyah, who had the expression of a woman who seriously needed a drink. Or a vacation.

"I'm going to need some context here."

Taliyah pinched the bridge of her nose and sighed. "It seems that when the coroner went to examine the body, the second he touched it with his tools, the 'body' fell apart into that mess you see in the picture." She gestured to the image of the pile of foliage and bark.

"So, wait." I flapped my hand in the air, thoughts whirling. "Wait, wait, wait. The body was glamoured? And the doctor broke the glamour accidentally?"

Taliyah's face pinched in frustration. "You

tell me."

I dragged the photos back towards me, looking over every detail. "I've heard about this kind of thing. Back in the day, when fae abducted humans, they would glamour a log, or an animal, or a bit of leaves and sticks to look like a dead body to leave behind, so people would assume that the person was dead and not look for them." I squinted, bringing the photo close enough to my face that my nose almost brushed against it.

"Did they?" Taliyah asked and seemed annoyed she didn't already know this, probably owing to the fact that she was fae. But, hey, that was hardly my fault! It wasn't like I'd placed her with a human family that had raised her.

"That kind of thing fell out of favor, even before I was born, though," I continued, before my attention returned to the images in my hand once more. "Wait." My arms dropped back to the table with a soft thump and I stared at Taliyah as the thought dawned on me. "Then this means, there's a chance that Bryony isn't dead, after all."

"That was what I was hoping you could tell me," Taliyah said, her eyes intense. "Though if this murder case just turned to a missing person case, I have just as few leads regarding who might have kidnapped Bryony Reid as I did on who could have killed her."

"Then you have no one?"

She cocked her head to the side and then shook it. "The few suspects I questioned, one was tight lipped, and the other almost wet himself when I started asking about Bryony."

I cleared my throat and dropped my eyes to the table, hoping Taliyah wouldn't notice. She wouldn't be exactly thrilled I was out questioning people on my own. She was right, though. If I couldn't think of any reason for Bryony to be murdered, then I had less ideas about why she'd be abducted. Especially in a really old fashioned fae kind of way. Not many people could pull off that kind of glamour.

Wait a second. What was it that Jackson had been blubbering about the night before? About having to break up with his fae ex-girlfriend in order to get married to Bryony? His ex-girlfriend who had, apparently, been devastated by the split? And had a very compelling reason to get rid of the competition?

A nymph with a grudge would be very capable of glamouring some leaves into a body. The only question was, what would she have done with Bryony herself?

"You've thought of something," Taliyah said, her eyes far too sharp as she stared at me.

I hesitated, but then figured I might as well

tell her. Sneaking around investigating was one thing. Lying to Taliyah's face was another, and she was liable to be a huge pain in the butt if she found out about it. Besides, I needed a ride, since my car was still out in the woods somewhere. Lorcan had pushed it onto the gravel shoulder to get it out of the way, but we hadn't had a chance to call for a tow the night before.

"I do have an idea," I admitted. "But if I share it with you, you are contractually obligated to not get mad at me."

That had Taliyah's eyes narrowing suspiciously, her face looking like a brewing thundercloud. "What did you do, Wanda?"

I grinned, unrepentant. "Rather than tell you, I'll show you. And you're driving, Chief Morgan."

Taliyah muttered something as she pushed away from the table, but I ignored her as I turned to go put something a little more appropriate on. I told her as much.

Lorcan was still dead to the world (pardon the pun), but he'd be waking up any second. That put a little fuel in me to get out the door, because I just didn't want to deal with whatever secrets he was so fiercely trying to keep. I figured I'd focus on bringing Bryony Reid home safe and sound, and if I got to punch someone in the process, then I guess good deeds really could be their own reward.

***

"I cannot *believe* you withheld information about an active investigation. Do you understand that I could arrest you for that?" Taliyah was still seething as she took the turn towards the greenhouse up on the hill.

I let her vent. Sure, she'd been at it for a while, and didn't show signs of slowing down anytime soon, but she wasn't making a move for her cuffs, so I wasn't paying much attention. Instead, I stared out the window without actually seeing any of the scenery.

I wasn't sure what we were walking into. Brooke the nymph was our best, and only suspect, but part of me was still struggling with the idea. Not that she couldn't have done it. Nymphs were fae, after all, usually members of Spring or Summer courts, and fae could be petty, jealous, spiteful creatures just like anyone else. One getting jealous and taking out a rival wouldn't shock me. Like, at all. It was the kidnapping aspect I was struggling with.

What would Brooke have done with Bryony after the fact? Keeping an adult werewolf contained somewhere wasn't exactly easy. And if Brooke had gone to all the trouble of making everyone think Bryony was dead and then stealing her away, what was the end goal? It couldn't be to kill her somewhere else, right? Why do the elaborate glamour route, then?

I hadn't had enough coffee to be thinking this hard this early. I leaned my aching head against the glass and closed my eyes.

"Are you even listening to me?" Taliyah asked, frustration in every word.

I didn't open my eyes. "Not particularly, no. Why? Did you say something new, or are you still going over how I interfered with an investigation and got you your only lead?"

There was a beat of silence before Taliyah muttered, "You're impossible."

I snorted. "You willingly married my cousin. You like impossible."

Taliyah let that one go, because it wasn't like she could argue with facts. She switched gears instead. "I can't believe Jackson wouldn't have mentioned a jealous ex he broke up with in order to marry the victim when I spoke to him. Who wouldn't bring that up in a murder investigation?"

Taliyah's car was very serviceable, but not very comfortable. I missed my leather seats dearly as I shifted around, trying to find a good position. "You just needed to get him drunk."

The sigh she let out was extremely put upon.

"I'm not even going to ask. If I don't know, I don't have to add it to the report."

The Green Goddess Garden Center had been empty for a long time before the current owners had taken over. It would have been impossible to tell that by looking at it when we drove up and Taliyah parked in the gravel lot.

Rows and rows of carefully tended flower pots, shrubs, and saplings stretched out behind the small glass fronted green house. There was even a pond with a fountain shaped to look like a woman in a short chiton style dress pouring water from an amphora, where a turtle was lazily sunning itself.

The air was filled with the scent of dozens of flowers, like a heady perfume, and fat, fluffy bees drifted lazily from blossom to blossom, golden pollen clinging to their legs. It was like a little slice of paradise inside the city, a hidden green gem. Even Taliyah looked impressed.

But then, I guess that was what happened when a group of Dryads and Nymphs worked together.

There was a woman out front, dressed in khaki overalls, somehow making it work. Her skin was a perfect honey brown color, like oak wood, and the hair she had twisted up into a knot at the back of her neck was deep green, marking her as a Dryad. She was humming to herself as she watered some flowers, stopping to whisper to each one as she passed.

The woman smiled when she heard our feet crunch in the gravel, the smattering of freckles across her nose crinkling up with the expression. "Hello, is there anything I can help you with today?"

Taliyah strode up, flashing the badge she wore clipped to her belt. "I'm looking for Brooke."

The Dryad's eyes widened at the sight of the badge, her smile faltering a little. "Brooke? She's in the greenhouse, seeing to the water lilies. Is something wrong?"

Taliyah smiled, and if she was going for reassuring, she missed it by a mile. "I just need to speak with her."

The Dryad nodded, but didn't seem too happy about it. She did get out of the way though and let us into the greenhouse proper.

If it had been warm outside, it was darn near tropical inside those glass doors. Sweat dampened my brow, and the air I inhaled was rich with the smell of green growing things and fresh water. There was soft lighting along the pathways, and fairy lights strung between some trellises, so it wasn't dark inside. It made everything softer, a little magical.

Towards the back, there was another raised

pond, turning the greenhouse almost into a grotto. This one was huge, filled with water plants, and the fountain was a gorgeous metal sculpture of a flock of birds in flight, with the water rolling over their wings and dripping down to the surface like rain.

A woman stood at the pond's edge, dressed in a T-shirt and cutoff denim shorts, her long blond hair pulled back into a ponytail that swayed gently as she worked. Her arms were underwater, almost to the elbow, as she did something to a cluster of lily pads and creamy pink flowers with pointed petals.

If I looked carefully, I could just see the hint of her pointed ear sticking up through her hair.

"Brooke?" Taliyah asked when we got close enough for conversation.

The blonde woman looked up, brows furrowed, but she smiled. "Yes? I'm sorry, have we me…"

Her words trailed off into a strangled squeak, and she straightened up, only to drop into a bow as soon as her eyes shifted to Taliyah.

"Princess Olwen! Please forgive me, I didn't realize it was you."

I'd never seen someone pale and then flush in such rapid succession. Taliyah cleared her throat, darting a look around as she flapped her hands at the bowing nymph. "That's not necessary. It's fine. I'm just here to talk to you."

Taliyah was as flustered as I'd ever seen her, and considering she'd faced down wicked faeries, scheming witches, and her own ex-husband, it was kind of hilarious that a bowing nymph threw her right off her game. I wondered if I could get a picture to show Maverick without her shooting me.

"Of course, Princess." Brooke straightened up and fixed her eyes on Taliyah. "What can I do for you?"

Taliyah took a breath and let it out slowly. I could practically see her counting to ten. "First of all... don't... call me that."

Brooke looked confused but didn't argue. Point for her. Taliyah, meanwhile, just stood there and I was fairly sure she was trying to wrestle her temper down. Well, I wasn't about to stand there, waiting for her. The humidity was doing things to my hair, and I wanted out of there.

"We actually wanted to talk to you about your ex-boyfriend. Jackson," I clarified when Brooke gave me a puzzled look.

"Oh. Jackson." Brooke shook her head. "What about him?"

Taliyah shot me a pointed look. "We actually wanted to talk about Bryony Reid. His fiancé."

Brooke looked puzzled, glancing between us. "Oh, yes. I was very sorry to hear of her passing. But I don't know what I could tell you about her. I never met the girl."

Taliyah nodded, like that was what she'd expected. "But when Jackson ended things with you to marry her, you must have been upset. Maybe hurt, or even jealous."

Brooke blinked at us for a moment, before her lips twitched, and that delicate, almost doll-like face crinkled up as she let out an ugly, snorting laugh. "Oh, my gods. Jealous? Over *Jackson*?"

Taliyah and I shared a look.

Brooke wiped at her teary eyes, trying to get control of herself. "Don't get me wrong, Jackson was sweet. Fun. But I'm more than twice his age, and I don't have any interest in settling down. Werewolves are almost hardwired to do just that. I wasn't upset about the 'break up', because... I mean, it wasn't even really a break up because it wasn't even really a relationship. Not in my mind anyway—it was always just a fling to me." She placed her hands on her hips, leaving damp marks. "Honestly, I would have called it off myself if he hadn't. He spent all our time together moaning about having to get married, and his parents pressuring him. And that got old really quick." Brooke glanced between us, looking contrite. "But I am sorry about Bryony. She seemed like a sweet girl. I hope you find the person responsible."

Well. It seemed that the echoing smack I could hear inside my head was Taliyah and I hitting another dead end. If the way she was holding her mouth was any indication, Taliyah felt the same way. She was still going through the motions, though. "Where were you on Friday night?"

"Here, actually." Brooke pushed a strand of hair back off her face with one hand. "We held a little party for when the night-blooming jasmine started. Just for some of our customers, a little wine, some cheese. Spring water for the rest of us."

That seemed like a solid alibi, and one easily verified, too. Ugh.

Taliyah tapped her pen against her notebook and then tucked both of them away in her jacket pocket. "Alright, thank you for your time. I'll be in touch if I have any more questions."

"Of course, Princess," the nymph chirped. "Anything you need."

LACE LAMENTS

Chapter Twelve

Taliyah grumbled something, but she didn't correct Brooke about the whole 'princess' title thing again.

She also didn't exactly run out of there, but she sure power walked. I had to jog to catch up, worried she might actually leave me there.

"Well, so much for that," I groused as I fastened my seat belt. "What's our next move?"

Taliyah turned to stare at me, her expression wavering between amused and outraged. "*Our*? There is no 'our'. I'm taking you home, and then I will continue with the investigation. And as soon as I figure out how to explain that the body exploded into leaves, I will have to inform Bryony's next of kin that she is, in fact, not dead."

"And after I got you a lead." I shook my head sadly, giving her a raised brow expression. "That's gratitude for you."

"Wanda, you make clothes. You're not a police officer."

"You bring Maverick along all the time," I rebutted, a little stung. "How is that fair?"

Taliyah raked a hand back through her hair, her eyes sparking icy blue. "Why are you arguing with me? Do you honestly want to go around playing detective?"

After a moment's thought, I had to admit that, no, I really didn't. I just wanted people to stop thinking I murdered a girl who wasn't even dead.

"Fine," I said as I sagged back into the seat and fished out my phone. "But I hope you understand the sheer amount of magical knowledge and skill that you're shunning."

Taliyah muttered something that sounded suspiciously like, "I'll live with it," but I decided to ignore her as she threw the cruiser in reverse.

I didn't really want to go back to the house. Especially since my car wasn't in what I would call 'driving condition'. It looked like it had been attacked by a rogue can opener. I figured I should call Lorcan to see if he'd arranged for a tow truck yet, or if I needed to do it. Granted, with the way he'd been acting lately, I wasn't even sure I should bother asking him if he'd already taken care of it. The likelihood that he had was extremely low.

The phone rang. And rang. And rang, and finally switched over to voicemail. I hung up, stabbing the button with more force than necessary. Great, no car, and Lorcan was who knew where. Home was sounding better and better, all lovely and isolated.

What in the world was up with Lorcan? He'd never ignored a call from me before. He'd been acting so odd lately, and it was really starting to worry me. He couldn't be getting bored with our relationship... could he? Is that what this was? Was he having an affair? The idea was so strange to me because it wasn't a thought that would occupy any other witch's mind. Witches didn't get attached to men. Men were there for sexual release and procreation, and that was it. Therefore, a witch didn't give a rat's ass if a man was cheating because she'd always beat him to it.

Lorcan had always been upfront in his pursuit of me. Even with the bond driving him to complete it in the early days, he'd made it clear that he wanted me, bond or no bond. And he'd wanted me as in he wanted Wanda, not just his Kiss returned to him. But what if that was all it was? Another kind of hunt. He'd enjoyed the chase, but now that he'd won me, now that the chase was over, was it time to look for the next thrill?

Lorcan didn't seem the type, but what the spell else was I supposed to think? He was never around anymore, always busy at 'the office'. There was that vanilla scent on his clothes. And this most recent situation—when he'd been all dressed up for no apparent reason. The fact that I hadn't pinned him in place with a hex and demanded some answers already said a lot—and mainly about how worried I was regarding what his answer might be.

I just couldn't figure it out. And it wasn't like I could talk to anyone else in the coven about it, because most of them didn't even believe in marriage. Well, there was Olga, but she was a complete romantic who had very little common sense when it came to men, and even if I got desperate and tried to talk to Taliyah, there was a chance the conversation would get back to Maverick, and then I'd have to set myself on fire.

But there was one person I *could* talk to.

"Actually, would you mind not taking me home?" I stuffed my phone back into my purse and straightened up. "Can you just drop me off at the old cemetery, instead?"

Taliyah gave me a very odd look, but didn't comment as she took the next turn that would take me in the direction of the duplex. She pulled up to the entrance of the cemetery and then turned to look at me.

"I'm not going to ask."

"Probably better you don't," I agreed as I opened the door, hopped out and waved, making sure I was mostly out of range as I added, "Call me when you need help solving the case."

I ducked behind an angel statue as a snow ball burst against its wing a second later, which had me cackling. I then watched the taillights of Taliyah's cruiser as it vanished in the distance. Facing the cemetery, I felt strangely home again. Like I was getting back to my roots. When was the last time I'd wandered through a cemetery in the dark? And cackling? Talk about living every stereotype.

I walked between the graves, dry grass rasping against my legs, listening to the night insects chirp, but I didn't head for the duplex. Instead, I turned towards the two-story farmhouse on the other side of the cemetery, where the windows were still lit up with soft golden light.

With its wraparound porch, and original siding carefully restored, the farmhouse was almost too cute to be tolerated. It looked like something someone had scraped out of a nostalgic painting, which made it almost perfect for its owner. All it needed was a porch swing and I might actually have started throwing up all over the wholesome mess.

I knocked once and waited. It didn't take long for the door to open and reveal Poppy with an honest to goodness dishtowel thrown over her shoulder. I hadn't thought people actually did that. Of course, I also couldn't remember the last time I'd dried a dish. In response, I looked at it and groaned.

Poppy gave her big, beaming smile of welcome, though her brows were pinched together in confusion. "Wanda! Hey, how are you? Is… everything alright?"

I wasn't sure what my face was doing to cause that last sentence to come out of her so tentatively, but I didn't dare answer, because all of a sudden there were tears burning at the corners of my eyes, and what the spell was wrong with me?

Poppy's face crumpled with concern, because she was soft and compassionate and the kind of person who could cry and not be mortified, and somehow, through a series of events even I didn't fully understand, she had become my best friend.

"Why don't you come inside?" she asked, gently, like I was some skittish woodland creature that might bolt away at a harsh word.

I sniffed, refusing to acknowledge that the world had gone a little blurry around the edges, and stalked past her without a word. I also decided to ignore the way my shoulders relaxed once she closed the door behind us, shutting everyone else out.

***

Poppy listened, because of course she did. She had me sitting at her wood kitchen table with a cup of chamomile tea, which didn't really do anything to calm me down, but it was nice to hold so that my hands had something to do.

I didn't get into the entire sordid mess, because I really didn't want to think about all of it. I only mentioned that Lorcan had seemed distant lately, and I wasn't sure what was up with him, and then she'd come out with some ridiculous bit of advice like 'talk to him', which was as absurd as it was unhelpful. Talk? About feelings? What was this, a sitcom from the fifties? Please.

When I finished talking and Poppy finished giving me advice, I wasn't really sure what to do with myself. I didn't want to go back to the coven house where everyone would be nosy, but I also didn't want to go home where there was nothing waiting for me but an empty house and thoughts about why a girl had gone missing and why someone would go to such extreme lengths to make everyone think she was dead. Poppy had let me be for a few minutes, and then had quietly gotten up to make a few phone calls while I pretended to drink my tea.

When she came back, she started rooting through her cupboards, pulling out glasses, then she'd ducked into the fridge, grabbing fruit and juices. I eyed her warily. She wasn't going to try and make a juice cleanse or something, was she? This wasn't some feelings-based activity, was it? Because I'd have rather eaten one of the glasses than do that. But once she pulled out an enormous bottle of vodka, she reminded me of just why she was my BFF, in spite of all the cheer.

Poppy had just finished setting up the cocktail bar when the first knock on the door came, and she walked over to it, letting Fifi and Bailey in.

"Oooh, I needed this," Bailey said, wandering into the kitchen and accepting the cocktail that Poppy pressed into her hand. "It's been way too long."

Before anyone could respond, someone else knocked and before anyone could answer it,

LACE LAMENTS

Darla let herself in calling out, "Hiya, dolls!"

She sailed into the kitchen, shaking back the dark hair that was finally growing out of the shoulder length bob she'd worn it in since the nineteen twenties. "Hit me with two shots of the giggle water, please an thank ya!"

She caught sight of me at the table, and stumbled a little bit before pasting an extra wide smile on her face. Normally, Darla could be a little much. I'd lived through the twenties, and even I didn't understand half the slang that came out of her. But once Poppy slid a Hex on the Beach into my hand, the purple drink smoking lightly, like fog dripping over my hand, I found that I wasn't bothered by anything much at all.

It had been some time since the Black Cat Cocktail Club had managed to get together, and as the low babble of female voices washed over me, I found myself relaxing back into my chair. It didn't hurt that my drink was perfect, a little spicy, a little sweet, with a kick of citrus at the end.

Fifi couldn't seem to stop smiling as she settled into her chair, occasionally checking her phone. If she got any happier, her skin was going to start leaking light all over the place. Ugh, it was kind of gross.

When she checked her phone for the

umpteenth time in ten minutes, Poppy nudged her shoulder.

"Roy?" she teased.

Fifi blushed, looking sappy and pleased and ugh.

I snatched one of the cherries out of the garnish bowl and plucked the stem to throw at her. "Do you have to sit there being all happy and in love? Some of us are trying to drink here."

Fifi stuck her tongue out at me and laughed. "Not that I'm complaining," Fifi said as she tugged her drink closer. "But what brought on this impromptu club meeting?"

"Oh, well." Poppy sat with her own drink, something that went from pale yellow at the top and darkened into a lurid orange down at the bottom. "I just thought it had been a while. And Wanda's having a bit of a rough week, so I thought it would be nice for all of us and alcohol to cheer her up."

She said it oh, so casually, just slipping it in there like she was innocent. But I was on to Poppy's wiles, and I wasn't about to go venting about my relationship problems to a crowd, so she could just manage her disappointment. Concerned faces turned my way, though Darla looked more like she was going to throw up.

"Rough week, doll?" she asked, her voice a little too loud. "That's the pits. What's the skinny?"

I glared. Poppy gave me a too innocent look and sipped at her straw.

"Well..." I might not have been wanting to spill my guts about my relationship, but that didn't exactly leave me with a dearth of things to vent about. So, I gave in, slumped back into my chair and started stabbing my ice with my little cocktail straw with extreme prejudice.

"I've kind of been investigating a murder. Except maybe it isn't a murder, after all."

Darla jolted like she'd been shocked. "Huh?"

Fifi choked on her drink.

Bailey leaned forward, almost putting her elbow into a bowl of lemon slices. "A *murder*? How does a murder turn out to not be a murder? And why are you investigating it?"

I tossed back my drink and spilled the whole deal out for them. The nightgown, the wedding, Bryony's 'death', all the investigating, and the fact that maybe Bryony wasn't dead at all, but that we still didn't know where she was or who would have taken her. The group listened quietly, and at one point, some glorious paragon of womanhood slid another drink into my hand.

"So, I still need to find Bryony to clear my name. Because werewolves keep trying to attack me, and my sales in the shop lately are abysmal. Who wants to buy some formal wear that might straight up kill you? If that girl doesn't turn up, I might as well pack my bags and move, because no one will ever buy a thing from me again."

Throughout the whole talk, Darla squirmed around like a three-year-old at lessons. She fidgeted, played with anything her hands could reach, and at one point laughed way, way too loudly at something that wasn't actually funny. I turned my glare her way, which was usually enough to get her to tone it down, but she seemed to be working really, really hard not make eye contact with me.

Weird. And when it came to Darla, that was saying something.

I shrugged it off and continued.

"I thought we had the whole thing sewn up, when Taliyah and I went to talk with Jackson's supposedly 'jealous' ex-girlfriend." I laughed bitterly. "What a joke that was. She probably hadn't even noticed when he'd broken up with her. So, now we don't have any leads, no idea where Bryony is, and no ideas on who would want to take her in the first place. Plus, Taliyah wants me to stay out of it, because I'm not a 'law enforcement official' or something."

I made my air quotes extra sarcastic.

Poppy stirred her drink, frowning a little.

"We should start inviting Taliyah to these things. Not tonight, obviously, she'd be busy, but maybe…"

Poppy trailed off when she noticed I was staring at her, incredulous.

"Can we worry about my disaster before we start modifying the guest list, please?"

She flushed pink all the way to her hairline. "Right, sorry."

Darla squirmed again and tossed back her drink before she spoke. "I mean, you ain't really looked into the dame herself, ya know? What if she had her own squeeze on the side? Sure, she was workin' to get leg shackled, but you really never can tell with people."

My eyes narrowed into suspicious slits. "What do you know?"

Darla laughed, high and shrill. "Me? Nothin'! Boy, it's hot in here." She slammed back the rest of her drink and then started putting gin away like it was water.

I didn't like pushing the issue, normally. But Darla clearly knew more than what she was letting on. And the fact of the matter was that my magic had brought her to life. Back to re-life. Re-alived her—I wasn't even sure there was a word for it.

My power welled up, lacing through my voice like smoke. "Darla. Tell me what you know."

Darla squeaked, her back going as stiff as a broomstick. "Tell you what?" she responded, flashing her long eyelashes at me and smiling prettily.

"Unless you want to die a second time, tell me what you know."

She dropped the smile and breathed out a long sigh as her attention shifted to the drink in her hands. "Well, I'm pretty sure I saw Lorcan stepping out with some dame," she then blurted, three octaves higher than her normal voice.

I froze, feeling like I'd just been kicked in the stomach. Of all the things I thought she'd have come out with, that hadn't been on the list. "What?"

She started flapping her hands, her eyes shiny like she was holding back tears. "They wasn't canoodling or anything, but they were real close, right? I kept bumping into them while I was dealing with some hauntings, cause they were sticking to real out of the way places. I didn't know what to think of it, Wanda. Part of me thought I should tell you, but another part probably thought you didn't want me pokin' my nose where it didn't belong."

My lips felt numb. I was going to be sick. "What did the woman look like?" I asked, my voice low.

"Now, Wanda, we don't know—" Poppy started, but I silenced her with a raised hand as I returned my attention to Darla, who somehow, got even more frantic. Her words came out like a fire hose, tripping over themselves as she tried to get them out as fast as she could.

"She was dressed up real nice, right. But she ain't no Sheba, not like you, Wanda. I'm sure it's nothing, it's just you didn't say anything, and then I didn't know how to tell you."

"Stop." The word came out without any strength. I felt like someone had stabbed me, and I was slowly bleeding onto the floor.

Darla's mouth snapped shut, and she looked down at her hands folded in her lap. "Sorry."

Lorcan out with another woman? I didn't know what to say. I didn't even know what to think. It had never even occurred to me beyond a random and fleeting thought that I'd engaged with for maybe a few seconds before I released it. I suddenly felt very stupid for that.

The mood, which had been lighthearted and full, deflated like a sad balloon. Everyone was looking at me with varying levels of concern, and it felt like acid on my skin.

I pushed my chair back from the table and stood. "I'm going to head out."

Poppy jumped up, just a little tipsy and stumbling. "Wanda, stay. Please, stay."

But I couldn't. That treacherous burning was back in my eyes, and I refused to spill even a single tear. So, I just waved Poppy off. "I can see myself out."

I could feel their eyes on me all the way to the door, but I didn't look back once.

Chapter Thirteen

I didn't have a car, and I wasn't really in a state to drive even if I did, so I ended up calling Marty, of all people, for a lift.

Marty was the closest a human could come to being a golden retriever, a relentlessly cheerful, optimistic person who was nearly constantly smiling and seemed to only want to help people. Unfortunately, he was my best chance of getting home, although as I slumped in the passenger seat of the hearse, part of me wished I'd just walked.

Marty was a graphic designer by trade, and a ghosthunter in his spare time. Lorcan paid him to drive the hearse around during the day because Lorcan was paranoid that someone was going to try to off him and, apparently, it's harder to off a moving target. Lately, though Lorcan didn't rely on Marty's services much, ever since we'd started cohabitating.

Marty's voice droned on as he told me some story about the last investigation he and his merry band of ghosthunters had done, and I let the tone wash over me without actually paying attention. It was fine, I just needed to make the occasional sound to make him think I was listening, even as I allowed my thoughts to drift.

Lorcan with another woman.

Just the thought turned my stomach, filling me with something between rage and terror. He wouldn't, would he? Darla had tried to make it clear that they hadn't been going at it or anything when she'd spotted them together, but then why would Lorcan hide it from me? Why not mention whatever he was doing, even in passing? Like he had when that dental hygienist had started getting flirty, and he'd had to lay down the line.

The only answer was, that he didn't want me to know about this one. And if that was the case, then the important question was, why? What was different this time?

I wasn't sure I wanted the answer.

Okay, what the spell? This wasn't me. Of course, I wanted an answer! And if Lorcan really was having an affair with another woman, he was going to tell me who, why, and, most importantly, why he'd lied to me. Extra busy, emergency at the clinic, my shapely behind. That man had some explaining to do, and pronto.

All the while though, there was this voice inside me that kept saying *'told you so'*. A voice that insisted I should have known better than to allow myself to be put into this position —that if I hadn't trusted a man, hadn't allowed him access to my heart, I wouldn't be feeling the way I was now. If I'd been true to my heritage and not allowed a man in, I wouldn't be hurting.

By the time we pulled into the driveway, I had a full head of steam worked up, and I hopped out and almost forgot to say an absentminded goodbye to Marty. Lorcan's car was in the driveway, the engine still ticking, so he must have just arrived home.

My magic was roiling inside me like a thundercloud ready to spit lightning by the time I got to the door. My heart was pounding and my breathing was coming in short rasps. It took every bit of control saved up from a hundred and forty-two years of life to turn the doorknob with my hands instead of blowing it right off its hinges. Even so, it still slammed against the wall so hard that it rebounded and I had to catch it before it smacked into me.

It just made me angrier. And the horrible knot of tears I refused to shed were now clogging my throat, and they didn't help, either.

Lorcan was still in the front hall, hanging up his coat when I walked in. He wasn't in his scrubs again, and if he tried to tell me that the circles under his eyes and his neatly pressed slacks and shirt were owing to a 'rough day at the office', I was going to turn him into an armadillo.

What was worse? I could smell that vanilla scent again, thick and creamy and obnoxiously sweet. Maybe it was time to clue into the fact that what I was smelling was another woman's perfume.

Lorcan had just turned to greet me, a tired smile on his face, and the fact that he could face me like nothing was wrong, that he could look me in the eyes, well, it just made me furious, because he was a liar, and a phony, and an… an… undead penishead! He was exactly what I'd thought he was when I'd first met him, before he'd tricked me with all his stupid good looks and charms.

Lorcan's smile died a quick death when I opened my mouth and demanded, "Who is she?"

He had the absolute gall to appear confused,

like he had no idea what I was talking about—a little wrinkle forming between his eyebrows. And I absolutely did *not* want to smooth it away with my finger.

"She? Who, sweetling?"

"Seriously? We're going to do it this way?" When he just looked more confused, I cocked my hip to the side and flipped up my index finger. "You're out at all hours." Next finger. "You miss dates and forget to call me." Ring finger. "You're lying to me about where you're spending your time." Pinky finger. "And now I get to hear from other people about how you've been seen around town with another woman."

I had to cross my arms so I wouldn't reach out and shake him. Furious tears burned in my eyes, and I knew if I blinked, they'd spill down my cheeks, so I forced myself to glare at him with everything I had instead. "So, how about you don't insult my intelligence, and tell me who she is and why you weren't man enough to tell me the truth—that you've been cheating on me!"

Lorcan stared at me, horrified. Well, he was a damned good actor—I'd give him that much. But that was all I'd give him. It just made the tears burn that much hotter, and if he was really stepping out on me, then I absolutely refused to shed any of them on this man's behalf.

"No, no, sweetling, it's nothing like that." He shook his head. "My God, it's nothing even close to that." He took a step forward, like he was going to reach for me, but thought better of it when I made a little warning sound in the back of my throat. He ran his hand through his hair instead.

"Wanda, please. Yes, I've been lying to you, and I'm sorry, but I promise you, I swear to you, it's not anything like what you're thinking it is."

He looked so haggard, like he'd aged ten years in a way I knew his body would never be capable of. I wanted to trust him, which meant I had to be careful. In my experience in the coven, the most sincere people were the best liars.

I stalked past him into the kitchen. No way was I having this conversation on the couch where we'd spent many an enjoyable evening. "You have ten minutes."

I sat at the mostly unused kitchen table, my back just as stiff as the chair, and my arms tightly wound around myself. It felt like if I didn't have a tight enough grip, my ribs might just crack apart around the jagged pain in my chest.

Lorcan sat, looking miserable. "Her name is Dorothy."

And my entire body just wilted. Dorothy.

"And there is nothing of any romantic or sexual nature going on between us," he insisted, shaking his head and laughing at the very idea. "Dorothy works for the vampire that has started taking over Portland," Lorcan continued. "A vampire who has been consolidating power since Rupert died."

Of all the things he could have said, I sure hadn't expected that. I blinked, taken aback. "Rupert? Then what the spell is Dorothy doing here, in Haven Hollow?"

I'd have something to say about a vampire trying to take over in Haven Hollow, and my vampire brothers would, too. Assuming this wasn't just Lorcan spinning yet another story to try to get out of the truth.

Lorcan slumped against the table, his elbows on the wood. "Apparently, there have been some rumors coming from the Hollow, regarding you not being a fully blooded vampire and those rumors have made it to Portland. Dorothy has come here to investigate and to make certain you really are a vampire."

My gut went cold. It had taken a lot of planning, and even more dumb luck to convince Rupert and his people that I'd been turned into a vampire while letting everyone involved walk away still breathing. Well, other than Rupert and a few of his lackeys. I'd thought his unfortunate end, and the show we'd put on about me being 'turned' had been convincing enough to make everyone leave us alone. But if what Lorcan was saying was the actual truth, then I'd made a mistake.

"I've been handling it," Lorcan assured me. His hand stretched across the table, like he wanted to touch me, but he pulled back, his fingers curling into a fist. "I've been distracting Dorothy as much as I'm able—giving her a bit of a run around, telling her that you are still new to the life and adjusting. I didn't want you to worry, especially not with everything else you had going on. I wanted to protect you, Wanda." He sagged, looking miserable as I narrowed my eyes on him, wondering if this was the truth, wondering if I could put myself on the line again by believing him. "I'm sorry, sweetling. I should have told you. I... well, I realize that now. But I wanted to spare you, and I've done the opposite." He sighed. "I promise you, Wanda, I would never, ever hurt you like that—I know it must look that way, but the thought that you could believe I would do that."

"It did look that way."

"I'm sorry," he said again and there was tenderness and truth in his eyes. "I don't know how else I can prove to you that you are the only woman for me, my love. And you always will be the only one for me."

I sniffed and managed to turn it into a derisive sound instead of a snotty one. He could be telling the truth. I wanted to believe he was, which was what made this situation all the more dangerous. I didn't think Lorcan would betray me. I wouldn't be with him if I thought he could or would. But I also hadn't thought he'd lie to me, especially not about something as big as the vampires sniffing around, trying to find us out.

I might not have been as opposed to becoming a vampire as I was two years ago, but I wasn't in any hurry, either. I loved my power. I'd worked hard for it. It was part of me, as much as my hair or my eyes, and turning fully meant giving that up. And now... well, I wasn't willing to give that up.

So, while one day I might make that decision, it was a decision that needed to exist between Lorcan and myself. Not anyone else. And I wasn't about to be bullied into it, not by anyone.

I searched Lorcan's face, and he met my gaze. His eyes were bloodshot, which I hadn't even thought was possible. He looked like he'd been running himself ragged, not out canoodling with some vampire femme fatal.

"You're an idiot," I told him.

He cracked a half-smile. "I'm well aware. I'm so very sorry."

The sick feeling that had been curdling in my guts turned into anger. "And in all of this, with you running yourself ragged, letting me think the worst—" I bit off the end of the sentence, grinding the words to dust between my teeth. A deep breath, and I tried again. "You didn't think to have a conversation about it with me? When using your words could have cleared this entire mess up?"

Lorcan looked gutted, the guilt plain as day on his stupidly handsome face. "I was trying to protect you. I'm sorry. You were busy with your work, and then you were investigating a murder, and I didn't want to dump more trouble onto your plate—I would have helped you with this whole Bryony incident, as well, but I have been so busy trying to keep Dorothy and the other vampires off your scent."

I crossed my legs, letting one foot bounce under the table. He'd made a good point, I hadn't exactly been sitting around eating bon bons the past few days. But I wasn't quite ready to be mollified, yet. "You're still an idiot."

"Agreed." He hesitated, wincing. "There's more."

Because of course there was. My eyes narrowed into dangerous slits. "Spill it, Lorcan."

He visibly braced himself, like a man about to face the firing squad. It didn't bode well for the rest of the conversation.

"So, the vampire who's taken over in Portland, whom Dorothy has been shockingly tight lipped about, is having a gathering in a few weeks to introduce him or herself. As Rupert's adopted child, I am expected to attend. And I will be expected to bring you with me. I've been trying to get out of it in a way that won't be instantly suspicious, but Dorothy is proving to be a bit difficult about it. So far, no luck."

Ugh. Vampire politics were the worst. But I'd blow up that bridge when I came to it.

First things first.

I met Lorcan's eyes, holding his gaze so that he'd get a hint of how serious I was. "You will never lie to me again, Lorcan Rowe. I don't care if you think you're protecting me or what. You will never lie to me again or I will walk away and I'll never look back."

"I won't. I promise I won't. I'm sorry, sweetling. I never meant for any of this to happen."

He looked so miserable, and it tugged at my withered black heartstrings. Staying put in my chair was getting harder and harder, because relief was making me almost lightheaded. He hadn't found someone new. He was still the man I knew he was, fangs and all. My lungs could finally inflate. Though, even as I stood and walked around the table, letting Lorcan pull me into his arms, there was a tiny kernel of doubt wedged up behind my sternum like a bit of black ice.

Then he was pulling me close, and holding me a little too tightly. I could tell Lorcan was trying to be gentle, but he was clutching a little too hard, and I was going to have bruises in the shapes of his fingers if he didn't ease up. He buried his face in my hair, pulling in a deep breath, like he was trying to memorize my scent.

"I would never do that to you, sweetling," he breathed against the side of my head. "Never."

I closed my eyes and leaned into his touch, letting myself believe him.

After a short, but comfortable silence, he spoke again.

"And not just because you'd hex my bollocks off."

That made me snort, and I jammed a finger into his ribs. "Damn right I would."

But I couldn't keep the smile off my face.

Chapter Fourteen

After Lorcan spent the last couple hours before sunrise making things up to me, I lay awake in bed for a long time afterwards.

He'd arranged himself on his back, so once he fell asleep, I could stay half-curled around him, with my head on his chest. I traced invisible patterns against his skin with one finger while I thought.

If Lorcan had been awake, he might have smiled and told me that it tickled, or even tugged my hand to his mouth to kiss my fingertips. But that wasn't what I was thinking about —instead, I was still turning our conversation from earlier over and over again in my head. I'd been so relieved that my worst fears hadn't come true, that Lorcan was just in it for the chase and now that he'd 'won' he was ready to move on to the next hunt, that I hadn't fully taken in what Lorcan had been telling me.

I didn't like it that the vampires were sniffing around again. With everything we'd gone through with Rupert, I'd hoped that it would buy us a little peace, at least a decade or so. But whoever this new vampire in charge was, he or she was clearly suspicious. Who knew what that meant for our little group way out in the Hollow. Especially with tensions between witches and vampires coming to a slow boil.

Not that the witches were thrilled about my Blood Witch status, either. I didn't think anyone would come out to try and kill me over it if my secret came out, but I also wouldn't have been surprised.

After not coming to an easy answer, I told myself we'd take what steps we had to, and we'd go from there. No use obsessing over it. I still couldn't quite bring myself to sleep, though. After the day I'd had, with the highs and far more lows, I felt restless, and a little on edge. It didn't help that talking to Brooke had been a bust. Jackson certainly seemed to have had an inflated sense of his own appeal. Who wouldn't have wanted to marry him? Ugh.

Bryony was still missing though, and while I didn't think Taliyah would go out of her way to share information with me about a police matter, which was, frankly, rude after all the effort I'd put in and the help I'd already given her. But I doubted she was having much luck figuring out where our missing werewolf had disappeared to.

I started replaying the evening over in my head, re-examining the conversations I'd had, thinking of them like a mirror that if I just turned it the right way, it would light up and I'd be able to see everything I'd previously missed.

And... I was going to have to call Poppy, wasn't I? She was probably all beside herself, just marinating in unnecessary guilt. I didn't like to think about everyone's faces when I'd left, the sympathy was hard to stomach. At least it hadn't been deserved.

And then, lying there, I had the most unfortunate, unsettling, downright disturbing realization.

Darla had been right.

Not about Lorcan, thank spell, but about something else. We'd been focusing on the people who might have wanted Bryony to disappear: her uninterested groom, his jealous ex, her father's rival. But we hadn't spent as much time looking at Bryony's side of things. Everyone had just been so obviously grief struck, that I hadn't been suspicious of her side of things. But hadn't they all been a little too quick to throw accusations and guilt my way? Especially the mousy mother...

Still, looking into Bryony's family didn't feel right. Weirdly, it might have if I'd still thought she was dead. People getting rid of unwanted children was, sadly, not something I was unfamiliar with. My own mother kicked me out of the coven when I was blooded, and she fed my two brothers to vampires to destroy their magic, so she didn't have to live with the 'shame' of having birthed warlocks.

But Bryony wasn't dead, she was missing, and I didn't think her family would banish her, especially when she was doing what they wanted by getting married. It was clear that they were more invested in her 'settling down and having cubs' than she was. So then, why?

Had they changed their mind on Jackson's suitability, and decided their daughter 'dying' was better than calling the whole thing off? I rolled onto my back and stared up at the ceiling, thinking. We'd talked to Jackson, and his former paramour, because they seemed the most likely suspects. But Darla was right, we'd been focusing on Jackson's ex, and hadn't really thought to ask if Bryony had one. What if the 'other woman' in this situation was in fact an 'other man'? Or I supposed the 'other' could also be another woman, if Bryony leaned that way.

So, then the following question was: did this jilted lover make off with Bryony, leaving a 'body' so that no one would look for her?

Or...

Hmm.

I needed some answers, and I had only a few places to get them that wouldn't end up with me getting bitten. As much as I hated it, I didn't have a choice.

But if Lorcan was right, and the vampires were sniffing around, then I'd have to stay put until the sun finally set. And with any luck, I'd actually manage to get some sleep before then.

***

Thanks to my girl on the inside, I managed to find the strange playground that 'all the kids have started hanging out at', pretty easily. I wasn't sure what was so appealing about lurking around a slide in the dark, but I supposed I wasn't today's youth, so I didn't need to get the appeal.

True to Sybil's word, there were quite a few teens and preteens slouching around, standing in small groups while also very obviously not using any of the playground equipment.

Including the two I was looking for.

I felt even weirder about approaching children in the playground as I had in the candy store (and at night, no less), but unfortunately, going to talk to them at home wasn't really an option.

Sneaking up on a werewolf, much less two of them, was actually pretty hard. I didn't have a lot of patience at the best of times, so a few muttered words and a flexing of my power had the shadows pulling closer, hugging tight, until I was close enough to speak to them.

Marianne winced, her gaze dropping to the sand under her feet. Casey Reid's face twisted into a ferocious scowl, which would have probably been really intimidating if she wasn't on a swing with her pink little sneakers kicking in the air.

"You again?" There was a little growl to her voice, her eyes glinting in the dark. "We don't want to talk to you."

Well. Backtalk. Maybe there was hope for this one.

"Yes, and I'll be sure to write about that in my diary and then cry myself to sleep tonight." I wrinkled my nose at the faux turf underneath the playground equipment. I'd worn closed toe shoes, but the grit was going to absolutely ruin the leather if I wasn't careful. "But I need to talk to you about Bryony."

Marianna winced and blinked, like she was trying not to cry. "Can you please just leave us alone?"

Okay, well, that made me feel like a bully. Which, I probably was being, but no one else was giving me a straight answer or any answers at all, so here we were.

I'd try to keep it short. "I just need to know if Bryony was seeing someone. Did she have a boyfriend?"

"Yeah. Jackson," Casey said, aggressive in her defensiveness.

"Jackson was her fiancé, but don't try to kid me. She was neutral about him, at best. I've had a stronger reaction about what kind of wine I'm drinking than she did about getting married." I turned back to Marianne, who still wouldn't look at me.

She fidgeted, tugging at the sleeves of her shirt, pulling them over her fingers. "She did have a boyfriend," she said quietly, like a confession. "A Summer fae from town. He was a faun. But when she got engaged, she broke it off, and he left town."

Casey, for once, wasn't butting in. In fact, she was oddly quiet, her hands clenched into fists.

A faun, hmm? They tended to be a little

wild, I could see one going out with a werewolf girl. With their goat legs and horns, they were pretty close to nature. They were also pretty good at glamours, so it would be easy for one to say, turn a pile of leaves and bracken into a corpse long enough to fool the family.

It sure would have been good information to know, say, a few days ago.

I tried not to sigh. Or curse. They were children, after all. "Look, can you tell me anything else about him? How did he handle the breakup? Did they see each other again? Where did he go? Was he angry with her?"

Casey set her jaw at a mulish angle. "Why do you care?"

Don't yell at children, Wanda, I told myself, using it like a mantra to beat back my temper. "Do you think I'd be asking if it wasn't important?"

She looked away and heaved a sigh, like I was the biggest trial she'd ever endured in all her years. I was almost impressed.

"They didn't break up. Not even after Alder moved to Portland. They snuck around, and they were really freaking out about the wedding. Bryony told him that she was trying to get out of it, and she was. And then one day, she just… stopped trying. She did what they wanted, and she stopped seeing Alder."

Marianne looked shocked. "Why didn't I know about it?"

Casey snorted. "Cause Bry knew you'd tell mom and dad if they asked you."

Marianne glared. "That's not true! I didn't tell them I saw him at the wedding, did I?"

"Wait, what?" I made a 'stop' gesture with my hand. "Back that up. Alder was at the wedding?"

Casey looked mutinous, and Marianne vaguely ashamed again.

"Y-yeah," the older girl admitted. "He was there with the catering staff. I figured he was trying to convince her to run away with him again or something. But then, Bryony was gone, and it all seemed really stupid."

I pinched the bridge of my nose, telling myself that I could not shake a child. Especially not a werewolf child. But, oh, Goddess, the urge was there. "And you didn't think to mention any of this last time?"

Marianne sniffed, tears brimming in her eyes. "You asked who'd want to hurt Bryony. Alder wouldn't hurt her, he loved her. And besides, she's gone, what does it even matter? Your questions are stupid and it's too late."

Well, I had absolutely no patience for any of this. There was a reason they never asked me to teach young witches; they'd all end up as newts.

Astrid was the one exception, but even so, I'd pawned off half of her lessons onto Poppy.

Well, there was one thing I owed them, even if I had no idea how they were going to take it. "Bryony is alive."

Marianne froze, before rolling her eyes up towards me. The little mouse was gone, it was the wolf in those golden eyes now. A low, threatening growl trickled from between barred fangs as she glared at me.

Maybe that had been a mistake after all.

She snarled, flashing her teeth. "You're a liar. How dare you?"

I was a witch, wielder of fantastic magical powers. I was also blooded by a vampire, which made me just a little bit faster, a little bit stronger, a little bit *more* than most people. But I did still have a sense of self preservation, no matter how atrophied, and I knew I had to be very, very careful for the next few seconds.

I met her eyes and didn't look away. "I'm not lying, Marianne. She's alive. And Casey knows it. Don't you, Casey?"

It was only when Marianne looked towards her sister that I let myself do the same.

Because, yes, there it was, in the younger sister's face. She was trying to hide it, but she was still young. She hadn't perfected her resting bitch face that most teenagers developed.

The lack of reaction had been what tipped me off. Casey had been the more aggressive of the sisters, ready to throw down with a witch to keep her sister from getting upset. But when Marianne had showed me her teeth, there had been nothing from Casey. Silence.

The girl wouldn't meet either of our eyes, looking away for the first time like she was guilty.

Marianne was wide-eyed, shaking slightly. The wolf was gone, all that was left was the girl. "Casey?"

Casey's shoulders hunched up around her ears, and her chin ducked towards her chest as her sister stared her down. It was like the two of them had suddenly swapped their personalities.

"Casey!"

The girl jumped.

Marianne stared at her. "Then it's true? And you knew. Bryony is alive, and you knew?"

At that point, I guess Casey decided that it was a little late to protest, so she very hesitantly nodded.

A low, ripping snarl tore its way out of Marianne's throat. Her eyes were all wolf then, teeth too long and too white in her mouth. "I'm going to kick your butt!"

And just like that, they were gone. Casey didn't try to negotiate, didn't try to talk her sister down. She just bolted like a champion at track and field, with Marianne half a step behind her.

Their sudden departure created a couple ripples through the other people in the park, but most immediately drifted back to whatever they were doing.

I shook my head. Kids.

It was fine. I'd gotten what I wanted.

LACE LAMENTS

Chapter Fifteen

The drive to Portland meant I was going to have to test my hypothesis and get out quick if I wanted to beat the sunrise home.

I was all for keeping up appearances, but not if it meant spending the day trying to sleep and not suffocate in my car trunk, even if I was driving one of Lorcan's more roomy cars. Hard pass.

I had to retrace my steps a bit from that long ago fabric shopping spree, and as I thought about it, Lorcan really owed me another one for the stunt he'd pulled. I couldn't even remember the name of the place, only the food I'd had there, which had actually been pretty good. There weren't a ton of places that could do a really good wrap without it getting soggy.

Sadly, the restaurant wasn't my main goal of the evening, though from the sounds coming from inside, Thursday night was a popular one for students. The place was packed. I probably wouldn't have even been able to get a table.

My chicken wrap dreams dashed, I took a glimpse in the windows, trying to spot a familiar face.

I must have gotten too close to the door, because a frazzled server doubling as a hostess gave me a wary look. "It's going to be about a forty-five-minute wait for a table."

She looked like she wasn't in the mood for small talk, so instead of beating around the bush, I decided to go for it and hope for the best. "Actually, I was just looking for Alder. He told me to meet him here."

She shoved her hair back off her face, barely looking at me. "He's probably in his apartment out back. Check there."

Goddess bless young people who didn't value other people's privacy. I slapped a smile on my face. "Yeah, good point. Okay, thanks."

And then I turned and wandered around the building before she gathered up enough energy to ask me any questions like: who are you, and why are you looking for Alder? Very inconvenient, those.

There was a set of metal stairs around the

back of the pub leading up to a door, probably an apartment if the bronze numbers hanging on it were any indication. I had to knock twice before there was shuffling inside, and the door cracked open.

I looked into the very side eye that stared out at me, and slapped a hand to the door so it couldn't be slammed in my face. "Hello, Bryony."

That stunned the girl enough that I managed to nudge the door open and step inside.

The place wasn't terribly large, but it seemed cozy and it was cleaner than I probably would have managed on my own. The kitchen and living room were all one, and a hall disappeared towards the front of the pub, probably the bedroom.

Bryony was paler than the white paint on the walls, her eyes blown wide as she stared at me, her arms wrapped around her midsection. I gave her a once over, but she looked to be in good health, glossy hair, a pretty pink and white sundress, no kinds of visible bruises. Though she did look like she was one hopscotch round away from a panic attack.

"Nice place." I turned towards her, one hand on my hip. "And you're looking well. Much better than I anticipated, what with you being dead and all."

Bryony swallowed hard.

The young man I'd last seen her with outside the pub came down the hallway then, toweling off his dark hair. In their apartment, he apparently didn't bother with the glamour, since there was a set of curling ram's horns on either side of his head, though his legs and feet below the towel wrapped around his waist looked human enough. That explained the glamour he'd been wearing at the wedding. It had been him I'd seen there, putting down a tray and hurrying off.

"Did you say something, Bry?" He caught sight of me in the entrance way, and stumbled to a stop. "Oh. Oh, crap."

I fixed them with one of my better witchy glares. "Busted."

Bryony hurried over to Alder and slid her arms around his waist. He straightened up, as tall as he could, but it was really hard to look intimidating with a towel wrapped around your hips, no matter how impressive the horns were.

Up until that moment, a part of me had wondered if I was way off base. Maybe Bryony really was dead, but something had been done to get rid of the evidence, i.e., her body. Maybe I was grasping at straws. They were all things I had to consider. But here she was, alive and well, and I wanted to choke her with her own hair.

I braced my hands on my hips, glaring them down. All the fury and frustration I'd been dealing with for days was simmering in my stomach, until I felt like I could have spit fire given half the chance. "What in spell were you two thinking? Were you even thinking? Do you have *any* idea the kind of problems you've caused? And for what? Because you can't tell your parents that you don't want to marry some guy you don't know?"

I could have lost my business, Taliyah was spending hours trying to find the killer of a girl who wasn't even dead, not to mention the grief and suffering her family was going through.

"You don't understand!" Fat tears rolled down Bryony's cheeks as she blinked rapidly. "You don't know what it's like for werewolf women. They were never going to let me be with Alder. They were going to force me into a life I didn't want! Force me to settle down with someone just so I could have cubs and then my life would be nothing other than being a good little wife, quiet and submissive. I had to get out."

That did sound terrible. Any witch would rather eat her broomstick than be tied down like that. If some man expected me to be his good little house wolf, he'd get a face full of claws.

But then, witches tend to raise their young up with certain expectations. I was sure Maverick, a warlock in a coven of witches who all believed they were superior to him simply because he was born male, would have had a great deal of sympathy for Bryony.

"It's not that they're bad parents, please don't think that." She wiped at her eyes with a shaky hand. "They want what's best for me. It's just that what they've decided is best, isn't what I want. And I knew if I dug my heels in and told them I wouldn't marry Jackson, then they'd ask why, what was wrong with him, and then I'd get the whole guilt trip, and the talk about how I'm not getting younger, and how my entire life's purpose is to have cubs, apparently, and I–" Her voice broke, shoulders shaking. "I couldn't. I just couldn't do it. So, I ran, and I made sure they'd never try to follow me. I'm sorry. I didn't mean to hurt anyone. I just needed to get out and make sure no one came looking for me. I just wanted to be free."

Alder hugged her to his chest with one arm, the other making a grab for the towel as all the jostling threatened to send it sliding to the floor. And I really didn't want that to happen. Talk about an uncomfortable situation.

It was all very sincere, but there wasn't any need for her to lay her life story at my feet. It wasn't like I was trying to convince her to go back and marry her sad lump of an ex-fiancé. Good riddance to him. She could ride off into the sunset with her faerie lover with my blessing, and only call home in order to send them all photos of her behind, for all I cared. I just wanted her family to stop thinking I'd murdered her, especially when she wasn't even dead. A living person is kind of irrefutable proof of my innocence in a murder investigation, after all.

But Bryony was obviously upset. I could see the fine trembling in her shoulders where she was clinging to Alder, like she thought I'd come to tear her from his arms like something out of a fairy tale. Those were all anti-witch propaganda, might I point out. Still, I didn't want them suddenly deciding to put up a fight, thinking I was the enemy. So, the whole situation might need a bit of a gentle touch.

I took a deep breath. Compassion. I could do that. Poppy practically breathed it. How hard could it be?

"You're right. I don't know what it's like to be a female werewolf." And thank the Goddess for that. "But I do know that *faking your own death* and then moving an hour away is a bone-headed idea."

Okay, so maybe understanding and compassion were harder than they looked. If I asked, maybe Poppy could give me some remedial lessons. Or I could just drag her around with me and point her at people who were crying. That option sounded much better, and less likely to get me cried on.

"Portland was just a pit stop," Alder of the slipping towel protested. "We're leaving in a couple days."

Bryony nodded, sniffling loudly. "We're going to move to one of the new Hollows, maybe Misty Hollow. Anywhere we can be safe and together, where no one knows us."

I didn't barf, and frankly, I felt like I deserved a round of applause for that. Spare me from the young and infatuated. Then again, these were also the kind of people who decided that running away and leaving a fake corpse was a stellar plan, so maybe I should have just been grateful they didn't pull a Romeo and Juliet level of nonsense.

I glanced down, mostly to avoid visibly rolling my eyes, and saw the glint of gold on Bryony's hand.

"Well." I eyed the ring. "Congratulations, I suppose. I'm not here to stop you or interfere in your relationship. Go. Be happy. Move to a new Hollow, be grossly in love with each other. But I'm going to have to insist that you let your family know that you aren't dead. It's going to be better coming from you than when Chief Morgan has to inform them that your 'body' disintegrated into foliage on the medical examiner's table."

Alder winced. "I'm not that good at glamours. I always have trouble when they touch metal," he said, sounding apologetic.

Bryony beamed up at him, her face radiant even with the tear tracks. "You did great."

Their sappiness was giving me heartburn. "If we could get back on track here? You can't leave your family thinking you're dead, no matter how annoying they are. Plus, Chief Morgan is going to be increasingly angry if you let her keep wasting police manpower searching for your killer, and trust me when I tell you, you do not want to be on her bad side."

Alder went pale, sweat beading around the base of his horns. As it should. Alder, as a faun, might belong to Summer, but that didn't mean that he'd want to tangle with Olwen, the heir apparent for the Winter throne.

And while Taliyah wasn't the type to break out her faerie princess authority, especially for a case, I was quite happy to wield it on her behalf. Especially if it put an end to this whole stupid farce. I wanted this drama over with because I was sure it wouldn't be long before Haven Hollow came up with some new nonsense for me to deal with. Not to mention my business couldn't handle a whole gaggle of werewolves spreading rumors about me, and trying to ambush me on dark roads. Not that Lorcan wasn't happy to spend money on me, but I needed my own things in life, as well. Things I'd worked hard for. Things I cared about. Things that made me me.

"I'll call them." Bryony clasped her hands in front of her chest. "I promise. Once we're on the road, I'll call them and let them know that I'm safe. I'll call Chief Morgan, too."

Well, that was probably as good as I was going to get, and frankly, if I had to stand there watching them cling to each other all starry eyed, I was going to have to hex something out of self-defense. But, just to be sure, I whipped out my cell phone.

"I need a picture of the two of you just in case you decide to skip out on your word," I explained.

Bryony nodded and the two posed as I took their picture—just to ensure that I could clear my name and so I could give the family back some of the peace of mind, in case Bryony didn't do it for me.

"Great. Glad you're alive. Enjoy your honeymoon or what have you." I turned and went for the door. I was pretty sure that sappiness wasn't contagious, and if it was, I was likely inoculated thanks to Poppy. But I also wasn't willing to take that chance.

Besides, I still had a long drive ahead of me, and nothing was going to hold back the sun. It was a good thing Lorcan's car could haul it when given the proper pedal motivation.

"Thank you," Bryony called out behind me.

I waved over my shoulder. I was thoroughly done with the whole situation, and I couldn't wait to leave rubber streaks on the road as I peeled out of Portland. If Lorcan called with another lame excuse to delay me, he was just going to have to turn into a bat and fly his butt to the city to pick up his own stuff.

Chapter Sixteen

Against all odds and my better judgement, Bryony actually came through with calling her family and letting them know that she was in fact alive, and married, and I couldn't help but be curious as to which they were more shocked by.

I only found out second hand, when a very contrite Mr. and Mrs. Reid dragged themselves into my shop with their proverbial tails tucked firmly between their legs. I told them I'd send them the picture I took of the two lovebirds, but they said they'd rather not see it. Shame, because it was a cute photo.

There were a lot of subdued werewolves creeping around town after that, though I was pretty sure that had less to do with me being innocent and more to do with the talk Taliyah and Maverick laid down about how vigilante justice would not be tolerated in Haven Hollow. I was told there were visual aids for that presentation. Sadly, Maverick didn't get any pictures for me.

Though, the guilt must have been getting to them all, at least a little, because I started having an abnormal amount of werewolf customers. And it was clear they were just buying things as some kind of reparation. Well, that was judgmental of me. Maybe that burly, fifty-year-old werewolf man bought a size three sundress and a shawl because he thought it would bring out the blue in his eyes and do nice things for his shoulders. Who knew?

Taliyah wasn't impressed by my poking into things, but considering how everything turned out, she didn't feel the need to read me the riot act, either. Case closed and all that. I think she was just happy she didn't have to wrangle furious werewolves anymore.

Poppy did eventually accept my assurances that everything was okay and stopped calling me five hundred times a day to apologize. I think she only bought it because I told her I demanded a do-over cocktail night. I did actually want one. It was still novel, being able to get together with a group of my peers and not have to worry one of them was going to poison or hex me the second my guard dropped.

But, most importantly of all, Lorcan and I finally got our makeup date night.

And no way was I letting him off easy. No movie night at the cinema, oh no. We were going all out with a night at a small theater just outside of town. The Black Lily Theater had only opened up a few months ago, but I'd been hearing rave reviews. Just perfect.

Perfect enough that I decided to break out one of my newest creations for myself.

I'd gotten the idea from a couture magazine, but then I'd gone ahead and made the dress my own. The bodice and sleeves were a gorgeous black lace that let my skin peek through in little glimpses. Though, I'd put in some lining to keep anything important from flashing. Still, the square neckline did fabulous things for my collar bones. The skirt itself fell to the floor in silky draping folds. It wasn't so full that I'd have spilled into other people's seats at the theater, but it was floaty and fun, and of course, just a bit witchy.

A smoky eye, a dark plum lip, and some hair combs to keep everything smoothed into place, and I was ready to go. And since there wasn't going to be much walking, I could wear some of my favorite, least practical shoes, with a higher heel and little silver accents that flashed when I took a step.

The way Lorcan tripped on the carpet when he saw me made the hours of effort worth it.

The Black Lily was just a short drive outside of Haven Hollow, and Lorcan spent the trip assuring me that I would love the play that they were currently performing. He'd kept it under wraps, claiming it was part of the 'surprise'. I figured that I'd trust him this once, but if it was a flop, I was picking date night for the foreseeable future.

The outside of the theater was certainly impressive. It had been given the face of an old manor house, all stone and wood and huge gleaming windows. Two and half stories high, it loomed over the parking lot, and only the lights that lined the garden path curling towards the front steps let me know the place was actually open at all. They must have put up heavy curtains in those windows, to keep the light from sneaking out.

Gravel crunched under foot as we made our way past the flower beds and a few slender aspen trees. I'd just started regretting my choice of shoes, no matter how gorgeous they looked on my feet, when Lorcan stopped dead, his arm going rigid under my hand where he was escorting me.

"Oh, *bollocks*."

"What?" I craned my head, trying to see what it was he was looking at. "What is it?"

He paused, took a breath he didn't need, and I could practically see him doing the calculations in his head: could we run back to the car before whatever it was spotted us? He was actually turning his body away, back towards the parking lot, but then seemed to think better of it.

"Do you remember how I mentioned Dorothy?"

I gave him a flat, unfriendly look. "Where are you going with this, Rowe?"

A nervous chuckle slipped out of him. "Well, when I spoke to her, I might have thrown out mentions of a few places for her to see while she was in town. I'll remind you that I was trying to distract her, of course. I never once for a second believed she might actually show up at any of those places. You understand that, don't you, Sweetling?"

"Is she *here*?" I craned harder, trying to catch a glimpse of the woman Lorcan had been running around town with behind my back. Noble intentions aside, I was still a bit put out about the whole thing.

Lorcan grabbed my arm. "Don't *look*! Ah, damn, she's spotted us."

I trusted Lorcan, most of the time. I wouldn't allow him near my blood much less my bed if I didn't. But I hadn't quite been able to shake the little knot of displeasure that he'd been off, running around town with this 'Dorothy' person and without my knowledge. It was silly, and juvenile, and I knew that. Telling myself as much didn't seem to help at all, but it did manage to make the whole thing just that much more irritating.

But suddenly, I was being offered a chance to size up the competition, so to speak. Even though there was no competition. At all. That didn't stop me from being grateful that I was dolled up to the tens (potentially even the elevens), wearing a dress that I'd both designed and enchanted to show off all my best features. Unless Dorothy was an undead super model, I wasn't going to have anything to worry about.

She'd better not have been an undead super model, or Lorcan wasn't going to survive the night.

I'd braced myself for anything, a blonde Hollywood looking starlet, a voluptuous red-head, a seasoned brunette, sultry in her confidence. What I hadn't been expecting, however, was a silver haired octogenarian who didn't come up past my chin. Yep, that was Dorothy. And she strolled right up to us in a hot pink track suit.

"Dorothy," Lorcan said, politely, if a bit

strained. "I see you decided to take my recommendation on the play house?"

Dorothy fixed us both with a beady eye. She looked like any other older woman, except that her back was very straight, and her teeth were flawless. She also wasn't wearing any kind of glasses, which made her stand out a little. But she was a bit shrunken, looking bird boned and frail underneath the polyester.

Dorothy made an expression that, on anyone else would have been a smile. It had just a bit too many teeth in it for comfort, and her eyes stayed cold, like little chips of granite in her wrinkled face. She was nobody's grandma, that was for sure.

Though, to be fair, my own grandmother would have been much more likely to poison someone than bake them cookies, so I couldn't really judge.

The thing I noticed the most about her though, was how she stank. Nothing bad, vampires didn't tend to have body odor, at least, not their own. But the woman reeked of vanilla perfume. Like she'd upended the bottle and poured it over herself instead of dabbing just a little on. No wonder Lorcan came home smelling like her, he'd have picked up that scent just from standing within five feet. Possibly even ten.

I'd never known anyone with cnhanced

senses that wore that much perfume or cologne. It made me wonder if there was something wrong with Dorothy's nose.

"It sounded like an acceptable way to pass the time."

Even her voice was rusted with age, though it was still strong. Dorothy reached up to pat at the bun her hair was pulled back into, and I could see that each of her nails had been painted the same shade of hot pink, until they looked like Day-Glo claws. She looked me up and down, her nostrils flaring wide enough that I was glad all she could probably smell was her own perfume.

"This is her, then?"

The absent, almost off-hand way she spoke about me right in front of me got my hackles up. I knew picking a fight with the woman sent to investigate us wasn't the smartest thing to do, especially when I was supposed to be a baby vampire, and not a butt-kicking High Witch. But boy, did it rankle.

Lorcan's smile grew a little more brittle. "Yes, this is Wanda. My Childe."

He reached out to take my hand where it was wrapped around his forearm, nails digging in. It probably looked like a protective gesture to Dorothy, but I knew what it really was.

Please, don't, that touch said. He was trying

to subtly hold me back. At first, I was a bit offended. Did Lorcan really think I was so uncontrollable that I was going to out myself, blow up our life together, because of one crabby old wench being rude to me?

Then Dorothy gave me another once over, and her face puckered up like she'd bitten into a lemon, and I thought just maybe Lorcan had a point.

I smiled, making sure to bare the sharpened points my eye teeth had become ever since my second blooding at the hands of Janeth. Dorothy actually raised an eyebrow at that, but she stopped looking at me like I was something she'd just scraped off her sensible orthopedics.

Finally, she grunted with something that wasn't quite approval. Maybe approval adjacent, though.

"The gathering is in three weeks. I'm sure I'll see you there."

That was directed at Lorcan, who gave her a pained looking smile.

"I'm certain you will."

Since I was standing beside him, half pulled into his body, I was probably the only one who heard Lorcan's muttered, "Unfortunately."

It took more effort than I was proud of not to laugh. I pressed my lips together to flatten them out, trying to take on a more solemn expression.

Dorothy nodded, ducking her head like a bird that had just spotted something small and wriggling. She turned to go, heading for the car park. She only paused long enough to say something over her shoulder.

"Make sure you bring her."

And then she was gone.

I guess she'd decided against the play after all.

There was a heartbeat of silence, and then Lorcan said, quietly but vehemently, "Bollocks."

"So, she seems nice."

Lorcan gave me the look my comment deserved. "She's a terrifying harridan with the personality of a starving vulture."

"I just said that." Honestly, without the fangs and the dietary restrictions, she might have slid right in comfortably beside some of the elderly witches I'd met. Of course, both sides would scream bloody murder if I'd made that comparison out loud.

Lorcan turned to face me fully, taking both of my hands in his. He studied my face for a long second. "Are you alright?"

I realized with some surprise that, yes, I was alright. It hadn't been a pleasant interaction, but no one had died, so it wasn't the worst. "I'm good."

"And you still want to see the play? We can just go home if you don't."

I glared at him, tightening my hands enough that my nails dug into his palms. "Lorcan Rowe, do you have any idea the amount of time and effort it takes to look this utterly fabulous? We are going to the play, we are going to have a good time, and everyone is going to get to see my glorious dress." It wasn't a promise, it was a *threat*.

Lorcan grinned, squeezing my hands far more gently. "Alright, then."

I nodded, satisfied, and we set off up the path.

We made it three steps before Lorcan opened his big mouth. "So… do you still think I have designs on this mysterious vampire in town."

I glared. "Shut it, Rowe."

He didn't shut it. "I mean, don't get me wrong, I'm not opposed to an older woman. She just seems a bit predatory for me. And for a vampire, that's really saying something. I'm just not sure it would work out between the two of us."

It was a struggle not to laugh, and I refused to give him that satisfaction, so I poked him repeatedly in the ribs, hard enough that a human would have bruised. He finally relented, chuckling like an idiot.

Of course, I wasn't about to admit that I'd been jealous or worried out loud. But that meant I also couldn't call him out for forgetting to mention that the woman looked like she'd been vacuum sealed and was older physically than a lot of bridges in the area. The jerk.

It did make me wonder what the spell was up with Darla's eyesight. But then, maybe when she was acting in her official capacity as right-hand vamp, Dorothy was more likely to dress up a bit, and the pant suits were for her personal time. And I hadn't exactly asked Darla to describe the way the woman looked—like if she was old enough to have witnessed cavemen first discovering fire.

When we finally stepped inside the Black Lily, it was like the rest of the world fell away. The interior was dim, full of velvety shadows, with the only illumination coming from a few electric wall sconces and some twinkling lights up near the ceiling that looked like the night sky. It made even the open foyer feel private and a bit hushed.

The carpet on the floor, dark with patterns of smoke and pewter woven into it, was plush enough that the heels of my shoes left little marks like stab wounds when I walked. I liked that more than was probably healthy. But then,

I'd always liked seeing that I made an impact.

There was a reception desk done in a black lacquer so shiny that it acted like a blurry mirror on the far side of the lobby, just before the doors. That close to curtain call, I was surprised it was empty, other than one theater employee in a dark shirt and a gray and silver vest patterned with a stylized lily. Though, the Black Lily didn't strike me as the kind of place you bought tickets on a whim at the last second, so they were probably just there in case guests needed help getting to their seats.

We passed a poster set out in a silver Art Deco frame, and I frowned as I read the title of the play we were about to sit through.

"Toil and Trouble?" I frowned. "Lorcan, please tell me this isn't just Macbeth with a new skin. The witch propaganda in that play had always gotten up my nose."

"I think it's bad luck to say the name in a theater. You're supposed to call it 'the Scottish play'. But, no. Not quite, anyway." Lorcan passed me the program he had picked up, a glossy little magazine with a picture of three women on the cover.

I grumpily flipped through it, only to realize that, yes, it was a Macbeth reskin as I'd feared. But this play was actually a retelling from the perspective of the witches. Hmm.

I laughed, I couldn't help it. Suddenly, I was very much looking forward to the evening.

"Alright, Lorcan. You got me. Lead on."

He didn't head for the main hallway to the theater doors, though. Instead, he took a smaller door to the left that led up a short flight of stairs. I almost complained, since my shoes were doing terrible things to my feet, but then he opened the door at the top and ushered me into a private balcony, and I forgot all about my poor mangled toes.

The box seat had only two chairs, both upholstered in midnight velvet, as lush and soft as a dream. There were little black lacquer tables on either side, perfect to rest a drink or a snack. It was like our own private little world, with an exceptional view of the stage down below.

I settled in, pleased when the chair almost molded to me with a small sigh. "Okay. This is pretty great."

Though, with all the excitement of getting here, and dealing with Dorothy, part of me wished we'd stopped for dinner first. I was going to be struggling not to let my stomach drown out the second act at the rate things were going. I was just shaking out my skirts when I heard the crinkle of a bag, and I glanced up, suspicious.

Lorcan was holding a package of flaming

hot cheese puffs, a snack I adored but would never admit out loud on pain of death. Of course, Lorcan had noticed, even though I always tried to hide it. He could probably smell the spicy cheese powder on me, even after I washed my hands.

"Where in the world were you hiding those?"

He waggled his eyebrows at me. "A gentleman has to have some secrets, Sweetling."

The seats were arranged in such a way that, with the arm rests up, it was actually more like a small couch. It meant that I could curl my legs up and snuggle into Lorcan's side with his arm around me while I nibbled on snacks and tried not to get hot cheese powder on my gorgeous dress.

We settled in to watch the play about three amazing, powerful women setting up an arrogant man for his own downfall, and I was determined to enjoy every minute of it.

Whatever troubles might drop on our doorstep, there would be plenty of time to worry about them later.

Tonight, was just for us.

~~~~

The End

Return to Haven Hollow in:
Enchanted Emporium
Haven Hollow #26
(*Occult Oddities*)
by J.R. Rain & H.P. Mallory!

If you enjoyed *Lace Laments*, please help spread the word by leaving a review. Thank you!

About J.R. Rain

J.R. Rain is the international bestselling author of over seventy novels, including his popular Samantha Moon and Jim Knighthorse series. His books are published in five languages in twelve countries, and he has sold more than 3 million copies worldwide.

Please find him at: www.jrrain.com.

About H.P. Mallory

H.P. Mallory is a New York Times and USA Today bestselling author. She has eleven series currently and she writes paranormal fiction, heavy on the romance! H.P. lives in Southern California with her son and a cranky cat.

To learn more about H.P. and to download free books, visit: www.hpmallory.com

Made in the USA
Columbia, SC
10 July 2025